THE FACE IN THE CEMETERY

Egypt, 1914. The outbreak of war in Europe casts ripples that can be felt even in Cairo. Gareth Owen, Mamur Zapt and Head of the Khedive's Secret Police, is given the unhappy task of rounding up enemy aliens. But in a land where the adoption of foreign nationality is a popular means of avoiding trial by an Egyptian court, determining who counts as a German proves contentious.

And then there's the face in the cemetery. A cat cemetery, at that. Who disturbed the mummified remains by placing a human corpse amongst them? Is the villagers' talk of a mysterious Cat Woman mere superstitious nonsense, or something more sinister?

Owen would prefer to leave these matters in other hands. He has a more pressing concern in the shape of missing rifles (missing? in war time?) and dubious gun-toting ghaffirs. Villages usually elect the local idiot as the ghaffir or watchman (who else would want to take on the brigands?), so what are these toughs doing here? Not to mention a heavily-armed thumb-sucking girl.

The face in the cemetery, though, refuses to go away, and Owen comes to realize that it poses questions that are not just professional but uncomfortably personal.

THE FACE IN
THE CEMETERY

A MAMUR ZAPT MYSTERY

Michael Pearce

HarperCollins*Publishers*

Collins Crime
An imprint of HarperCollins*Publishers*
77–85 Fulham Palace Road, London W6 8JB

www.**fire**and**water**.com/crime

Published by Collins Crime 2001
1 3 5 7 9 8 6 4 2

ISBN 0 00 232698 1

Set in Meridien and Bodoni
Typeset by Rowland Phototypesetting Ltd
Bury St Edmunds, Suffolk

Printed and bound in Great Britain by
Clays Ltd, St Ives plc

1

Over towards the Nile the light shimmered and seemed to fall apart, and then it came together again and presented a beautifully clear picture of the river, with palms shifting gently in the river breeze, a pigeon tower, and children playing around a water buffalo in the shallows; so clear that you could make out every detail.

Only it was not a true picture, at least, not of this part of the river. The Nile bent away at this point and where the mirage was, was just scrub and desert.

The desert was playing tricks here, too, inland a quarter of a mile. Heat spirals danced away across the sand and dust devils chased among the graves, where galabeahed men stood silently, watching him.

'You're not a pet man, though, are you?' said McPhee.

'No.'

'I'm dogs, myself.'

Only it was cats here; dozens and dozens, hundreds and hundreds of them. They lay in open circular pits, uncovered by the archaeologists and then abandoned. Each pit was about eight feet in diameter and five or six feet deep. The cats lay on ledges around the sides, except that when space had run out they had been piled carefully on top of each other in the middle. Each cat had been tenderly mummified, the body treated first and then swathed in yards and yards of linen bandages. The pits stretched out towards the horizon.

'They weren't really pets, though, were they?' said Owen.

'Someone must have loved them, to lavish such attention on them.'

'But didn't you say –?'

1

'There are lots of inscriptions to the cat goddess round here, it is true,' McPhee conceded.

'So perhaps they were just running wild in the temples?'

'I don't know about running wild,' said McPhee severely. 'Fed, and not ill treated, perhaps.'

'But hardly pets.'

'Perhaps not.'

'Objects of devotion?'

'Sacred, certainly.'

But in the grave at Owen's feet there was something which was clearly not an object of devotion. It lay across the middle of the pit and cat mummies had been clumsily pulled off the shelves and spread over it in an attempt to hide it. It was rather longer than a cat mummy but bandaged tightly like them.

Except at the head, where the district mamur, alerted by the village omda, had uncovered enough of the modern bandages to reveal that the body was that of a twentieth-century, fair-headed woman.

'Identification?' said Owen.

'They all know her. The omda –' began the mamur.

'Someone closer.'

'There is a husband,' said the mamur, almost unwillingly.

'Husband?'

Owen looked at his papers. They made no reference to a husband.

'Where is he?'

'Up at the factory.'

'Has he seen her?'

'He knows,' said the mamur evasively.

Owen bent over the body. Already, in the heat, it was changing.

'You'd better get it moved,' he said.

The mamur nodded, and beckoned to two of the villagers. 'Mustapha! Abu!'

They came forward reluctantly.

'Wait a minute!' said Owen. 'Aren't you going to . . . ?'

He stopped.

2

'Yes?' said the mamur.

Owen shrugged. It wasn't really any of his concern and out in the provinces things were done differently; when they were done at all.

'It doesn't matter,' he said.

'Is there a hakim?' asked McPhee.

In the provinces any autopsy was usually conducted by the local doctor.

'He has been sent for,' said the mamur.

The two villagers were hesitating on the brink of the pit.

'Get on with it!' said the mamur. 'What are you waiting for?'

'We don't like it,' said one of the men.

'It's nothing. Haven't you seen a body before?'

'We're not bothered about the body,' said the other villager. 'It's these.'

He gestured towards the mummies.

'They're bodies, too.'

The men still hesitated.

'Look, they're only bodies. The bodies of animals, what's more.'

'We still don't like it.'

'They're not even recent bodies,' said the mamur persuasively.

'All the same . . .'

'Are you going to do it or aren't you?'

The answer, unfortunately, was probably not.

'Look,' said the mamur, 'if I move the cats, will you move the woman?'

The men looked at each other.

'If you move the ones on top –'

'And put them back in their right places –'

The mamur jumped down into the pit and began putting the mummies aside.

'Satisfied?'

The two looked at the other villagers.

'We call upon the world to witness that it wasn't we who interfered with the grave.'

'We witness, Mustapha!'

'Right then.'

The two got down into the pit, picked up the body of the woman, tucked it nonchalantly under their right arms and set out across the desert towards the sugar cane.

'Are you coming up to the house?' asked the mamur.

'We ought to check the identification, I suppose,' said Owen.

It was probably being over-punctilious. When he had arrived in Minya the day before and presented the mudir, the local governor, with the list of names, the mudir, knowing most of them, had gone through them mechanically, ticking almost every one. It was only at the last one that he had stopped.

'There's been a development,' he said.

He had gone to the door of his office and called in the mamur, sitting uneasily outside, and had shown him the list.

'That one,' he had said, pointing. 'Wasn't that the one . . . ?'

'Yes,' said the mamur. 'She's been found,' he said to Owen.

'Found?'

'Found dead. This morning.'

'Are you sure?' asked Owen.

'Would you like to see her? You could come with me. I've got to go back.'

'Perhaps I'd better,' decided Owen.

The mudir put a cross against her name.

'Is she worth the journey?' he said.

The path to the house led up through long plantations of sugar cane. The cane was twelve feet tall and planted so densely that the long ribbon foliage of one plant intertwined with the leaves of the next, making an impenetrable jungle. You could not see as much as a yard from the path; only the sky overhead, and the path itself, winding, not straight, and stubble underfoot.

Yet it was not the sudden loss of light, the hemmed-in feeling, that became troubling after a while, but the heat. The cane caught the sunshine and trapped it, so that, hot though it was outside the plantation, out on the open desert

4

by the graves – well over a hundred degrees Fahrenheit – it was hotter still inside. In no time at all Owen's shirt was sodden with perspiration.

McPhee took off his helmet, mopped his forehead, and swung the hat at the flies.

'Of course,' he said meditatively, 'there's the Speos Artemidos at Beni Hasan.'

'What?' said Owen.

Used as he was to the heat of Egypt, this walk through the sugar cane was leaving him quite dazed.

'The Cave of Artemis.'

'Really?'

'Artemis is the Greek version, of course,' said McPhee.

The sweat running down Owen's forehead was beginning to sting his eyes. Maybe McPhee was right. He took off his sun helmet too.

'Greek version?' he said.

'Of Pakhet.'

Packet? What the hell was McPhee on about?

'The cat goddess,' explained McPhee. 'The one those mummies were probably dedicated to.'

'Oh.' And then, after a moment: 'You think there could be a connection?'

'Well, Beni Hasan's not far from here, is it? There could even have been other temples nearer, of course. The whole area is noted for the special recognition it gives to Pakhet.'

It was the kind of curious information in which McPhee excelled.

'Fascinating!' said Owen heartily.

'It is, isn't it?' agreed McPhee with enthusiasm.

And totally irrelevant. It had probably been a mistake to bring McPhee. The Deputy Commandant's eccentricities were more easily containable in Cairo; but Owen had been desperately short of the right people for this sort of job.

It had probably been a mistake coming out here anyway. Why hadn't he just accepted the mamur's word in Minya and left it at that?

The path began to lead upwards now. The incline was slight but in this heat quite enough to make him break out in another shower of sweat. The mamur, too, stopped to mop his face.

Suddenly, from somewhere ahead of them and to the right, two shots rang out.

Owen looked at the mamur.

'Abdul,' said the mamur indifferently.

'Abdul?'

'The ghaffir.'

'What would he be shooting at?' said McPhee.

The mamur shrugged.

'Brigands.'

'Brigands!'

'We have them here. They live in the cane.'

'Can't you root them out?'

The mamur shrugged again.

'It's not so easy,' he said.

Again, it wasn't Owen's concern. Nor McPhee's either. The Cairo Police Force was quite separate from that of the rest of the country. He could see that, all the same, McPhee was wondering.

'Are there many of them?' he asked.

'About forty. They come and go. At the moment they're led by a Sudanese.'

'What do they do?'

'Rob. Protection.'

'The sugar factory?'

'The factory's got its own ghaffir. That was him shooting just then. No, mostly it's the villages. Crops, cattle, that sort of thing. If you want them left alone, you pay the Sudanese.'

'Don't the villages have ghaffirs too?'

The mamur laughed. Owen could guess why. The village watchman, the ghaffir, was normally just an ordinary villager, paid a piastre or two a month for his extra duties and armed, if he was armed at all, with an ancient gun dating back to the wars against the Mahdi. You could hardly expect him to take on forty brigands single-handed.

But the local mamur, the District Inspector of Police, surely he would have men he could rely on?

The mamur saw what he was thinking.

6

'It's not so easy,' he said again, defensively. 'We've tried beating the cane, but they just move to another part. It goes on for miles.'

'I can see the problem,' said McPhee, with ready sympathy. He fell in beside the mamur and they continued up the path together, discussing the different difficulties of country and city policing.

Owen was left with something nagging him, however. For the moment he couldn't identify what it was. It continued to worry away at the back of his mind as they walked up to the house.

In fact, there were several houses; neat, European-style bungalows with verandahs, gardens and high surrounding walls over which loofah trailed gracefully. Away to the right was the sugar factory, a long barn-like building with steam coming out at various points. In front of the building men were unloading cane from trucks and feeding it on to a continuous belt that led into the factory.

A European came up to them and shook hands.

'Schneider. I'm Swiss,' he said, as if making a point.

He glanced at the mamur.

'They've just brought the body up,' he said.

'Has Mohammed Kufti arrived yet?' asked the mamur.

'One of my trucks brought him over,' said Schneider. 'He's in the house now.'

'We'd better go over,' said the mamur.

'Drop in for some coffee when you've done,' Schneider said to Owen. 'My wife will be glad to see you. She doesn't get much chance to talk to Europeans.'

The mamur led them over towards the houses. The one they wanted was not part of the main cluster but set a little way back and native Egyptian in style: white, mud brick, single-storey, with an inner courtyard and a high surrounding wall. Inside, it was dark and although the room they were led into was empty, somehow there was the suggestion of many people off stage.

There was a piano in the room, a surprisingly good one, which looked used and well cared for. Little bowls of water, still half-full, were set beneath its feet. It had not escaped the usual ravages of the termites, however. In several places beneath the piano there were small piles of wood dust.

An Egyptian, dressed in a dark suit, came into the room and shook hands.

'Kufti,' he said. 'I'm the doctor.'

'Found anything yet?' asked the mamur.

'I haven't really started. Some things are obvious, though. She was poisoned. That was almost certainly the cause of death. There are one or two tests I have to do, but that is consistent with the symptoms and there are no apparent injuries.'

'What was the poison?' asked Owen.

'Arsenic.'

The usual. Especially in the provinces, where poisoning your neighbour's buffalo was an old established custom.

'Can you cover her up?' asked the mamur. 'We want the husband to identify her.'

'He's seen her already,' said the doctor. 'Does he have to see her again?'

'For the purposes of formal identification,' insisted the mamur.

The doctor made a gesture of distaste and left the room.

The mamur went out and then came back and led them along a corridor and into a small room where, in the darkness, a man was sitting hunched up on an *angrib*.

'Come, Aziz,' said the mamur, with surprising gentleness. 'It is necessary.'

Aziz? For some reason Owen had not taken in that the husband was Egyptian.

They went into another room, where the woman was lying on a bed, covered up with a sheet. The doctor turned the sheet down. The husband broke into sobs and nodded.

'That's all,' said the mamur reassuringly.

'Come with me, Aziz, and I will give you something,' said the doctor.

'How can it be?' said the husband brokenly. 'How can it be?'

*   *   *

8

'I'm Austrian,' said Mrs Schneider, smiling prettily; quite.

'And your husband's Swiss.'

'That's right.' They both laughed.

She led him out on to the verandah, where coffee things had been laid out on a table. A moment or two later Schneider joined them, with McPhee. They had dropped behind so that Schneider could take him into a room and show him something he'd found near the cat cemetery.

A servant brought a coffee pot and began helping them to coffee. The aroma mixed with the breeze that had come up from the river and spread about the house. They could see the river, just, over the sugar cane. The breeze had come across the cane and by the time it reached them was warm and sweet.

'Of course, I didn't know her well,' said Mrs Schneider. 'She kept herself to herself. Or was kept. I used to hear the piano playing, though.'

'All the time,' said Schneider. 'Music, I like. But not all the time.'

'I didn't mind it,' said Mrs Schneider. 'She played beautifully. Anyway, she didn't play all the time.'

'It seemed like it.'

'She's played a lot lately.'

'What sort of music did she play?' asked McPhee.

'German music.'

'Lieder?'

Schneider looked at his wife.

'Sometimes,' she said. 'Brahms, I think, often.'

'I suppose there will have to be an investigation?' said Schneider. 'Or won't you bother?'

'There will certainly be an investigation,' said Owen. 'But that will be conducted by the mamur. Neither Mr McPhee nor I do that sort of thing.'

'Not down here, at any rate,' said McPhee.

Schneider looked at Owen curiously.

'I thought you did do that sort of thing,' he said.

'Only if there's a political side to it,' said Owen.

The role of Mamur Zapt was roughly equivalent to that of the Head of the Political Branch of the CID. Only in Egypt, of course, there wasn't a CID. The nearest equivalent to *that* was the Parquet, the Department of Prosecutions of the Ministry of Justice. The Parquet, though, was Egyptian and the British Administration, which in effect ran Egypt at that time, kept it at arm's length from anything political.

'You wouldn't call this political?' said Schneider.

'Not at the moment, no.'

'I thought that was the reason why you were here . . . ?'

'That's quite different. The two are completely separate. From the point of view of the law, murder is a civil crime and will be treated as such; that is, investigated by the civil authorities.'

Mrs Schneider flinched.

'I suppose it must be murder,' she said. 'Only, hearing it said like that – '

'Of course it's murder,' said her husband impatiently. 'What else could it be?'

'I just thought that, well, you know, when I first heard about it, and heard that it was poison, well, I thought – '

'What the hell did you think?' said Schneider.

'That it might be suicide.'

'How could it be suicide? She was bandaged, wasn't she? And in the pit. Did you think she walked there?'

'Well . . .'

'Suicide!'

From somewhere out beyond the immediate houses, in the direction of the house they had just left, came the sound of a mourning ululation starting up.

Mrs Schneider flinched again.

'It doesn't seem right,' she said. 'Not for her.'

'It's the family,' said Schneider. 'You wouldn't have thought they'd have cared enough to bother.'

Owen knew now what it was that had been nagging at him.

'I heard some shots,' he said to Schneider, as they were walking back out to the truck.

'Oh, yes?'

'The mamur said it was your ghaffir.'

'Very probably,' said Schneider.

10

'What would he be shooting at? The mamur said brigands.'

'We do have them. Not as often as he claims, however. I think sometimes he just blazes off into the cane.'

'That's a service rifle he's got.'

'Yes.'

'I was surprised. Ghaffirs don't usually have that sort of gun.'

'They've all been issued with them round here.'

'Not just your ghaffir?'

'No, all of them. We had to get one especially so that our ghaffir wouldn't feel out of it.'

'Whose bright idea was this?' demanded Owen.

'The Ministry's. We had an inspector down a few months ago.'

'Well, I think it's crazy. Putting guns like this in the hands of untrained people like –'

'Oh, they're trained, all right. Musketry courses, drill, mock exercises, the lot.'

'Ghaffirs?' said Owen incredulously.

It didn't square at all with the picture he had of the usual Egyptian village watchman, who was normally much more like Shakespeare's Dogberry.

'Yes. It's the new policy of the Ministry, apparently.'

'Well, I still think it's bloody crazy.'

Schneider shrugged.

'Maybe you're just out of date,' he suggested.

Maybe he was, thought Owen, as he drove back to Minya in one of the company trucks, lent for the occasion.

But now it nagged at him even more.

Trucks were still new in Egypt and it was the first time he had ridden in one. He wasn't sure that he liked it. The sensation of speed was disturbing and it was very bumpy. Once they had left the cane behind them they were driving across open desert. There was no real road and they were thrown about heavily. He and McPhee both put their sun helmets on to protect their heads when they hit the roof. What with the unfamiliar motion, the constant jolting and the fumes from the engine, he began to feel more than a little queasy. He saw that McPhee's face was looking increasingly strained, too.

Still, it certainly got you there quickly. He glanced at his watch. At this rate they would soon get to Minya and with any luck would be able to catch the afternoon boat.

'Have you got them all now?' asked the mamur.

'I think so.'

'Except for her, of course.'

'Ought we to have something in writing?' asked McPhee.

'To say she's dead?'

'If we don't, she'll stay on a list somewhere and that could cause endless trouble.'

Owen looked at the mamur.

'Will you be sending in a report?'

'Report?' said the mamur, as if it was the last thing that would occur to him.

'She's a foreigner. You have to file a report.'

The mamur looked very unhappy.

'Certainly, certainly,' he muttered.

Owen guessed there was no certainty at all.

'When you do, I'd like to be sent a copy.'

'Of course!' said the mamur, even more unhappily.

The party was already assembled on the landing stage. Some had bags, some had cases. A little group of spectators watched curiously.

'That it?' asked Owen, as he went down on to the landing stage.

A police sergeant came forward and saluted smartly.

'That's it, Effendi,' he said.

A woman suddenly broke away from the group, rushed up to Owen and held out her hands.

'Take me!' she said frantically, waving her hands in front of him. 'Take me!'

'You're not German, are you?'

'I'm married to one. That's him, there. You can't take him and not take me. He's my husband!'

'I'm sorry,' said Owen. 'We're only taking Germans.'

'But I'm married to one! That's the same, isn't it? We've

been married for forty years! You can't take him and not take me!'

'I'm sorry.'

He hated this. He hated the whole thing. It was not what he had come into policing for. But then, when he had first become Mamur Zapt, Head of the Khedive's Secret Police, there hadn't been a war on.

2

War had come to Egypt like a bolt from the blue. Looking back, Owen could see that there had been plenty of signs that it was coming, but at the time he, like everyone else in Egypt, had not taken them seriously. He had put them down to the infantile war games that the Great Powers were forever engaging in, manoeuvres which were merely ritual. And then, suddenly, barely more than a month ago, the manoeuvres had turned out to be not merely ritual.

What had made it even more of a surprise was that no one in Egypt had been paying much attention. The declaration had come during the hottest part of the year, when everything in Egypt had closed down. Most members of the Government were on holiday on the Riviera. Those British officials whose turn had come round had left for England. Egyptian officials had headed for the coast. Kitchener himself, the Englishman in whose hands most of the strings of power in Egypt lay, had departed for Europe; for which relief Owen, who had not got on with the Consul-General, had been giving much thanks.

The great Government offices were largely empty, their occupants having migrated, like the rest of the population of Cairo, to the cafés, where the Mamur Zapt, confident that in the extreme heat even the most desperate of criminals would not be thinking of crime, tended to join them.

And so when the news hit Egypt it did not at first really register. After the initial shock, Egypt had shrugged its shoulders and got on with doing what it normally did in August. That is, nothing.

But then the first orders began to arrive from London and

among them was the instruction to arrest, detain and place in internment all German nationals and other suspicious foreigners. In the cafés, unkind Egyptians asked if that included Englishmen.

Owen had hardly got into his office when he heard the phone ringing; and he had hardly got it into his hand before the person on the other end was speaking, or, rather, bellowing.

'Owen, is that you? Look, this is damned silly! They've taken Becker.'

'Becker?'

'Sluices. He's the one who knows about sluices. Do you know about sluices? No, I'm not surprised. Not many do. They're tricky things. And once you've got someone who knows about them, you don't muck him about! What is more, you hang on to him. Because if he goes, you won't find another.

'Now this chap's really good. He's been working for us for fifteen years. It's got so now that I can't do without him. With him gone, the whole bloody system will close down. Sluices, dams, then the lot.

'How would they like that, then? You tell me. The whole country depends on water, the water depends on the dams, the dams depend on the sluices and the sluices depend on – yes, you're right: this man Becker!'

'I take it he's German.'

'Of course he's German! Or something. What the hell's that got to do with it? He does his job, like everyone else. Only much better, that's the point.'

'Yes, I know, but there's a war on, and there's this policy of intern –'

'Sod the war! The whole system will collapse, I tell you. Look, Owen, you've got to do something, make an exception . . .

'You can't? It's nothing to do with you? Then who the hell is it to do with? Don't tell me. I know. It's London, is it? I might have guessed. Well, look, you can bloody tell London –

'Yes, I know, but they'll listen to you more than they will

15

to me. I'm just a stupid engineer, just someone who makes everything work. You've got the gift of the gab, their gab –

'They won't? All right, talk to someone here, then. How about Kitchener? He's not entirely without sense, have a go at him –

'He's not here? He's in London, too? I might have bloody known it! Look, there must be someone you can talk to about this man of mine –

'All right, all right, I know there's a policy of internment, and it's got to be general, I can see that. But surely it can be applied sensibly? Surely people can be reasonable, surely you –

'Why should you be an exception, Owen?!'

He decided, nevertheless, that he ought to do something. Calls like this were coming in all the time. He took his helmet and went across to the Consulate to have a word with his friend, Paul. Paul had been one of Kitchener's ADCs and was now the Oriental Secretary.

He found him in Kitchener's office; sitting indeed, in Kitchener's chair.

'At last!' said Paul, with a dramatic sweep of his hand. 'They held me back, but now I've made it!'

'You're not really in charge?'

'Cunningham is nominally.' Cunningham was the Financial Adviser. 'But, as always, the reality of power is different.'

He wriggled in his seat.

'Just trying it out for size,' he said. 'I find it a little small for me.'

'All right, if you're really in charge, there's something you can do. It's this damned internment policy.'

'Laid down by Whitehall,' murmured Paul. 'Can't touch it.'

'What I want is power of discretion. That wouldn't solve everything, but it might help.'

'Discretion is normally understood,' said Paul. 'You've got to leave some latitude to the man on the spot. However . . .'

He thought about it.

'However, I'd be a bit careful about it, if I were you. Have

16

you read the newspapers lately? The English ones? They're full of spy scares. There's all sorts of panic at home and some of it is spilling over here.'

'Yes, but –'

'And then there's another thing: they're making changes. They're bringing some new people out here. One of them is something to do with security.'

'That's my job.'

'Sure. I expect he'll be working to you. But, Gareth, he'll have contacts back at home and he, too –' he waved his hand again – 'might be wanting to try other people's seats. I daresay he'll be no problem, but you see what I mean when I say that you ought to be a bit careful just at the moment.'

'Don't use too much discretion – is that what you're saying?'

'That, and also that you ought to get some kind of formal approval, in writing, of your powers.'

'You can give me that, can't you?'

'Yes. But I think it would be better if it came from Cunningham.'

'OK, I'll try and have a word with him.'

The bar at the Sporting Club was much less crowded than it usually was at lunch-time. This was because so many people were on holiday. Owen had been hoping to find Cunningham, but he wasn't there. However, he did find someone he knew from the Ministry of the Interior, a man named McKitterick.

'Guns?' McKitterick said, leaning his arm easily on the bar. 'Well, yes, and not before time. Look what the ghaffirs had to make do with up till now.'

'Yes, but these are service rifles. You don't want to put them in the hands of untrained men.'

'They won't be untrained. We've got a big training programme going.'

'Yes, I've heard about that. But it's the wrong sort of training. It's military training.'

'Isn't that what they need?'

'Ghaffirs? Village watchmen? Mostly they shoot crows.'

17

'But sometimes they have to shoot brigands, and when they do, they've got to have a weapon decent enough to put up a show with.'

'Very rarely, only in some parts of Egypt, do you have to fight brigands. And when you do, you don't want ghaffirs doing it. You want police or soldiers. It's a confusion of functions, from an administrative point of view. A ghaffir's function is much more limited.'

'Yes, we know about confusion of functions, thank you,' said the other man, nettled. 'And we know about ghaffirs, too. Look, we've gone into this very thoroughly, more thoroughly, I suspect, than you have, and the conclusion we've come to is that there is a need to do something about the ghaffirs. Both in terms of training and in terms of weaponry. One of our inspectors looked into this in great detail and came up with a really first-class report.'

'Which suggested turning ghaffirs into a sort of internal army?'

'If that's the way you want to put it, yes.'

'Answerable to whom?'

'The Ministry, of course.'

'The ghaffir used to be answerable to his own village.'

'And still will be. But there's a need for wider co-ordination. Look, you've just come back from Minya, haven't you? What chance has a single ghaffir there got against a pack of brigands?'

'You use the police. Or the Army.'

'I think, Owen, that the Army's got other things on its mind just at the moment. And the whole point of this is to take some of the load off the police. I really don't see what it is that you've got against reforming an antiquated, inefficient, and frankly useless service.'

'It's just that I don't like the idea of a well-armed, militarily trained force of fifty thousand men operating independently in the country at a time when it's at war.'

McKitterick stared at him incredulously.

'God, Owen, what's got into you? "Operating independently"? It's not operating independently, it's operating under us. Do you think the Ministry's going to launch some kind of coup? You must be crazy! Aren't you taking a perfectly sensible reform a little over-seriously? Perhaps you've been working too hard. Why don't you just stay out of the sun for a day or two?'

When he got back to his office he found that Nikos had pushed to one side the lists he had been working on and put in a conspicuously central position on his desk the memorandum from Finance that he had been trying for several weeks to ignore.

We first wrote to you some seven weeks ago requesting an explanation of how your apparent disbursements under Headings J, P, Q and Y of your Departmental Expenditure Statement are to be reconciled with the figures you give in Section 5 (c) ii and 8 (g) iv, not to mention Financial Regulations (see Sections 4 (d) i, 6 (b) v and 7). Despite requested requests . . .

Didn't these blokes know there was a war on? Hadn't they realized that people might have something better to do than answer their potty memoranda? And how could anyone be expected to answer a memorandum that might have been written in Pharaonic hieroglyphics for all the sense he could make of it?

He pushed the memorandum indignantly aside.

'There's been a man phoning from the Ministry of Finance,' said Nikos, watching from the doorway. 'He says he'll try again.'

On reflection, Owen thought he wouldn't speak to Cunningham about discretionary powers. Not just at the moment.

He had recently moved into a new apartment in the Midan Kasr-en-Nil. Zeinab had moved in with him, which was a considerable act for a woman in Egypt at that time. It was a considerable step forward in their relationship, too, and Zeinab had doubts about it. Every time he came home he half expected to find her not there.

She wasn't there now. However, her things were still scattered about the flat so he decided that it wasn't permanent. He poured himself a whisky soda, took a shower and then went out on to the balcony, from where he could see right across the Midan to the Nile on the other side. He was watching the amazing sunset when Zeinab arrived.

She took off her veil and kissed him. Then she helped herself to a drink and came out on to the balcony.

'Something terrible's happened,' she said.

'Oh, yes?'

'They've taken Alphonse.'

'Alphonse?' He knew the names of most of Zeinab's friends but couldn't remember an Alphonse. He didn't sound like an Egyptian. Perhaps he was a new artist friend?

'I'd made my appointment as usual, but when I arrived he wasn't there. Gerard said they had come and taken him that morning. I blame you.'

'Me?' said Owen, astonished.

'You're arresting them, aren't you?'

'Is he German?'

'No, he's a perfectly normal Levantine. However, he became a German because someone was chasing him for a debt. Or was it a woman who wanted to marry him? Breach of promise – yes, I think it was breach of promise. But he's not really a German at all and I don't think you should have arrested him.'

'He's down on a list, I expect.'

'Can't you take him off it?'

'Well . . .'

'Nikos could do it. Nikos is good with lists.'

'Look, it's not any old list, it's a list for a purpose, and its purpose is the identification of German nationals so that they can be interned.'

'But he's not a German, as I keep telling you. He just *became* a German, and he certainly wouldn't have done that if he'd known you were going to arrest him. I told him at the time that it wasn't a good idea. He ought to have become a Panamanian or something, and then no one would really know what he was.'

20

'Panamanian wouldn't do. Panama doesn't have consular privileges.'

Under international treaties imposed on Egypt many foreigners had so-called consular rights. Among them was the right to be tried not by an Egyptian court but by a court set up by the consul concerned, usually in another country and at a time far distant; which made possession of foreign nationality in some cases highly attractive.

'If you can get him out,' said Zeinab persuasively, 'I'll see he becomes something else.'

Nationality was a loose concept in Egypt. It could be acquired simply by recourse to a local consul, plus, of course, the payment of an appropriate sum; and brothel-keepers and the owners of gambling dens tended to change nationality with astonishing frequency.

Egyptians were cavalier about nationality partly because there was so much of it about. Egypt was one of the most cosmopolitan countries in the world. One eighth of the population of Cairo was foreign born and the proportion was even higher in Alexandria. Greeks, Italians, French, Albanians, Montenegrins and Levantines of all sorts jostled shoulders in the narrow Cairo streets. The Khedive himself was Turkish. And then there were the British, of course.

The British kept themselves very much to themselves. They worked alongside the Egyptians, but outside the office they seldom met. A few people – Owen, himself, for instance – had Egyptian friends, and the people at the Consulate, Paul especially, mixed socially with upper-rank Egyptians. But to a very considerable extent the two nationalities kept apart.

If this was true of the men, and true, too, of the women for that matter, it was especially true of relationships between men and women.

An Englishman could be in the country for years and not meet an Egyptian woman. He would rarely meet an Italian, Greek or Levantine woman either, since all round the Mediterranean men kept a peculiarly jealous eye on their womenfolk; but in the case of Egyptian women it was even worse.

They were perhaps no longer confined to the harem as in the past (only the rich could afford harems these days), but instead were relegated to some dark back room, from which they only emerged heavily veiled and dressed in a long, dark, shapeless gown that revealed nothing of the woman underneath.

They were never seen in public. If they went out, say, to do the shopping, they would be accompanied by a servant who would zealously defend them against any exchange with a man. If, rarely, they went to some public place such as a theatre, they would sit on separate, screened benches. If their husband received guests at home they would stay out of sight.

Young men of any kind, not just British, had a hard time of it and possibly would not have survived had it not been for the obliging ladies in the streets off the Ezbekiya Gardens.

In the case of the British, extra help came annually in the form of 'the fishing fleet', as it was known, the arrival of dozens of young women from England for the start of the Cairo season. One effect of this, though, was to reinforce the existing social division between the British and the Egyptians, which was almost complete; and Owen never ceased to give thanks that very early in his time in Egypt he had had the good fortune to meet Zeinab.

It had come about through a case involving her father, Nuri. Nuri was a Pasha and, like most of the old Egyptian ruling class, French-speaking and heavily Francophile in culture. Partly in reflection of this, and partly, it must be admitted, from his own idiosyncrasy, he had allowed his daughter a degree of latitude quite unusual in Egyptian circles. He saw no objection to his daughter meeting Owen; and, once met, things had developed from there.

Zeinab had established her independence to such an extent that quite early on she had acquired a flat of her own, where she lived, she assured her father, very much *à la française*. Nuri, impressed, had acquiesced; not, perhaps, quite comprehending that even in Paris at this time for young women to live on their own was not entirely *comme il faut*. In this unusual setting it had been possible for the relationship between Zeinab and Owen to develop; and over time it had developed very strongly.

Lately, however, they had begun to notice just how much time. They were both now over thirty and were becoming aware that many of their friends, even those as young as themselves, were getting married. They wondered whether they should do so too.

Here, though, they came up against that division between Egyptian and British, a division that was not just social but brought with it all the extra baggage that went with nationality: race, religion, customs, expectations and assumptions. And this was especially true when one of the nations concerned was an occupied country and the other the country that was occupying it.

It was not actually forbidden for a member of the Administration to marry an Egyptian, but there was a kind of invisible wash of discouragement. It manifested itself in all kinds of ways: questions about whether it would be possible for a person holding a post like Owen's to be seen to be impartial if he were married to an Egyptian (no one else in Egypt thought the British were impartial, anyway); sudden shyings away in the Club; the frown of the Great (which was one of the things Owen had against Kitchener).

On Zeinab's side, too, there were all kinds of cuttings-off: political separation from her artist friends, many of whom would see her as having gone over to the enemy; social repudiation by many of the circles in which Nuri moved and which she had grown up in; and, perhaps above all, an alienation from Egypt itself and a mass of Egyptians actually unknown to her but from whom she was reluctant to distance herself.

And yet, in the end, it was the walls inside themselves, not the obstacles outside, that were the problem. Or so they were coming, tentatively, to think. But those, argued Owen, were things they could do something about. They could try to work themselves through them. And somehow, by what chain of reasoning they were not entirely clear, this had led to their decision to move into a new apartment together.

Zeinab, Owen knew, remained far from convinced about

it; but then she had a lot more to lose. Owen himself, aware of the extent to which she felt herself vulnerable and exposed, was beginning to think they ought not to leave things like that for too long. Whatever their doubts about themselves, they ought to resolve things one way or the other.

And, besides, he was coming to think, might not this be their chance? Surely, with Kitchener out of the way and everyone's minds on the war, a private exercise of discretion – well, yes, you could call it that – might go unremarked; or if not quite unremarked, at least without having the same degree of significance attached to it as in more normal times.

Still unhappy about the issue of service rifles to ghaffirs, he rang up the Ministry and asked if he could see a copy of the inspector's report.

'By all means,' said the Egyptian civil servant he spoke to. 'It's rather a good one, actually.'

And when it came round, Owen could see why people were impressed. It was immensely thorough. The inspector had visited lots of districts – Owen recognized the references to Minya – and gone into great detail. Certainly, from what he said about Minya, he appeared to have a good grasp of the nature of the ghaffir's work and the sorts of local problems that he faced. The analysis was respectable, the arguments well set out, and the conclusions appeared to follow from the arguments. The only thing was that they were daft.

He rang up the Ministry again and got the same obliging Egyptian as before.

'About the Report,' he said. 'Do you think I could have a word with your inspector?'

'Fricker Effendi? Certainly.'

He hesitated, however.

'Is there some problem? My interest is of a departmental nature. I have already spoken to McKitterick Effendi about it.'

'No, no . . . It's just that, well, Fricker Effendi is no longer available.'

'No?'

24

'No.' The official hesitated again. 'As a matter of fact, I understand that you are holding him.'

'I am holding him?'

'Yes. He has been taken into internment.'

3

A little to Owen's surprise, for he had not expected it so soon – indeed, he had not really expected it at all – he found next day on his desk the copy he had asked for of the mamur's report on the German woman's death. When he looked at it, however, he was less surprised. It was perfunctory in the extreme, merely reporting the death of a foreign national, female, and the discovery of her body in one of the graves of a local excavation.

The report had been sent, as was customary, to the Parquet, which was responsible, in Egypt, for investigating all deaths in suspicious circumstances, and a Parquet official had scrawled 'Noted' on the copy and initialled it before sending it on to Owen.

Owen wrote back asking to be kept informed of further action in the case.

He was out of the office for the next two days – taking more wretched people into internment – and when he returned he found a further communication from the Parquet. All it consisted of, however, was his own letter returned to him with, at the bottom of the page, in the same negligent handwriting as that on the mamur's report, the words 'Referred to the Department of Antiquities'.

Owen picked up the phone.

'Why the Department of Antiquities?' he demanded.

There was a little pause.

'Wasn't it something to do with an archaeological site?' said the voice on the other end indifferently.

'It was to do with a body. Found on one.'

'The Department of Antiquities handles anything to do with desecration of sites –'

'And the Parquet handles anything to do with bodies.'

'Not old ones, not archaeological ones.'

'This is a new one. Not archaeological.'

'Are you sure? It was found –'

'If you look at the report you will see that the mamur refers to the body of a German national. Were there German nationals in Egypt in Pharaoh's time?'

There was another pause.

'Perhaps it had better be looked into,' said the man unwillingly.

'Perhaps it had. And the Consulate notified.'

'The German Consulate has been closed,' said the man triumphantly.

'But another Consulate will have taken on the job of looking after the interests of German nationals remaining in the country.'

There was an audible sigh.

'Please continue to keep me informed,' said Owen.

In the shops at least there were signs that there was a war on. The prices of all imported goods rose sharply. The rise in the price of petrol didn't affect many people since there were still very few cars in Egypt and only the rich had them. But the rise in the price of paraffin was a different matter. The poor used paraffin for both heating and cooking (wood had been scarce in Egypt for years) and were hard hit.

The rise in the prices of imported goods Owen could understand, but those weren't the only prices that rose. The cost of flour and sugar went up too and they were things that were produced locally. He had only just seen sugar cane growing in huge quantities down by Minya. He couldn't understand it and nor could the ordinary Egyptian. The newspapers were full of complaints and charges of profiteering.

They were talking about this one evening in the Officers' Mess at the Abbassiya Barracks. The regiment was leaving for Europe the following day and Owen had been invited for a farewell drink.

27

'It'll mean problems for you,' said his friend, John, one of the Sirdar's ADCs and someone who had been a useful contact at Army Headquarters.

'Why him?' asked one of the other officers.

'Because the man in the street will become restive, and he's the one who will have to keep order when we've gone.'

'Thank you for pointing that out,' said Owen. 'However, in one way things should become easier: there'll be fewer drunken soldiers around.'

'Ah, yes,' said someone, laughing, 'but the Australians will be here instead. Or so the rumour goes. You might do better to come with us.'

There was a general laugh.

'Where do you stand, actually, Gareth?' asked John curiously. 'You're on secondment, aren't you?'

Owen had served with the British Army in India before coming to Egypt.

'It started as secondment,' said Owen, 'but then I applied for a transfer. And after that it became permanent.'

'So, strictly speaking, you're a civilian now?'

'That's right.'

'Yes, but with your experience –' said John.

'You were up on the North West Frontier, weren't you?' asked one of the other officers.

'For a while, yes.'

'Just the sort of man we need.'

The thought had occurred to Owen, too.

The Parquet official had obviously taken heed of Owen's observation – perhaps it was the mention of the Consulate that had done it – for in the mail the next morning was a copy of the letter he had sent to the mamur at Minya. It asked him to supply further details of the 'incident' in the cat cemetery. In particular, it asked for details of any damage to the site – a thrust at Owen, this? – but also the cause of death.

McPhee's mind, too, seemed to have been on the cat cemetery that morning – possibly because he and Owen were on their way to intern some other unfortunates – for, as they were passing the House of the Kadi, just after noon, he glanced at his watch and said:

'Shall we go in? And have a look at the cats?'

'Cats?' said Owen.

'Yes. They bring the offal just about now.'

They went through an ancient ornamental gateway into a beautiful old enclosed courtyard. Sure enough, a servant was just emerging from the Chief Justice's house carrying a large bowl. He threw the contents on the ground and at once dozens of cats emerged from all corners of the courtyard and began to tuck in.

'It used to be a garden,' said McPhee. 'The Sultan Baybars set it aside specifically for the use of cats. Over the centuries the garden was built on, but the custom of feeding the cats has survived. Only now, it's the Kadi that does it.'

'The Kadi feeds the cats?'

'That's right. I think the Prophet was fond of cats, or perhaps he said he was, once.'

They turned back and through the gateway.

'I know this is Muslim,' said McPhee, 'but am I fanciful, do you think, to see a continuity from that cemetery in Minya? That was Pharaonic, of course, but often later practice has its roots in some earlier custom, and it would not be surprising. What do you think?'

Owen had absolutely no opinion on this at all and they continued on their way up the Darb el Asfar.

They had almost reached the Bab-el-Foutouh when McPhee said:

'You know, Owen, about that business at Minya: there are a lot of things that trouble me. That poor woman, of course, and how she landed up there. Horrible! Just think of how her husband must feel! And then those brigands. You really would have thought that the local police would have eliminated them by now. And then those shots! Surely, arming the local ghaffirs is not a sensible way of dealing with such problems. I really do feel you should speak to someone.'

'I have.'

He told McPhee about his conversation with McKitterick.

McPhee listened intently.

'Have I understood you correctly, Owen? The ghaffirs are being issued with new service rifles, brought together and trained to operate as some kind of independent force?'

'An independent army, I called it.'

'But under whose command?'

'The Ministry's, apparently.'

'Owen, I find this rather disquieting. Does the Sirdar know? What does he, as Commander-in-Chief of the Army in Egypt, think of another army operating independently in the country?'

'Well, it's not quite like –'

'And under foreign command, too?'

'Well, hardly foreign. It's the Ministry –'

'But, Owen, you know as well as I do what the political situation is like here. Sadly, not everyone is on our side. There are some here – politicians –' McPhee spoke the word with disdain, 'who question the relevance of the war from an Egyptian point of view. Is the Minister among them?'

'Well, I really don't know –'

'But, Owen, it is important to know. Where does he stand? Could he be playing his own game?'

'Look, he's got McKitterick right by his side –'

Every Minister had an English 'adviser' alongside him. It was one of the ways in which the British made sure that the Government was going in the right direction.

'But, Owen, he could be pulling the wool over McKitterick's eyes!'

'McKitterick's not daft.'

Although, come to think of it, this new policy with respect to the ghaffirs was not very bright.

McPhee tut-tutted impatiently.

'Owen, where did the idea come from? The Minister?'

'Well, I think it came from one of the inspectors, actually. He went into it and wrote a report –'

'An Egyptian? Close to the Minister?'

'A German, actually.'

'A *German*!'

'Yes. McKitterick thinks very highly of him.'

'German! But, Owen, we are at *war*! Are you seriously telling me that we are allowing an independent army, fifty thousand strong, to roam the countryside under the command of a *German*?!'

Despite Owen's attempts to straighten him out, over the next few days McPhee kept returning to the matter.

'Yes, I know, Owen. I realize that, strictly speaking, he was not in charge. But, surely, it is very likely that, having written the report, and it having been received in such glowing terms, he would be given responsibility for implementing it. And if he was responsible for implementing it, then –

'Yes, I realize that even if he was given responsibility for implementing it, he wouldn't be able to do anything now because he is in an internment camp. But there may be others in the Ministry – the Minister himself –

'No, I am not bonkers! Look, the report was accepted, wasn't it? And implemented. That means there must be support for it inside the Ministry. I really do feel – '

Then one morning he stuck his head triumphantly in at the door.

'Owen, I have been looking at the Departmental Handbook, and do you know how many Germans there are in senior posts in the Ministry of the Interior?'

'No.'

'Six!'

McPhee came right into the room.

'Doesn't that say something about the Minister's sympathies? Six! How do you explain that?'

It was, in fact, a little on the high side for a single Ministry. There were plenty of foreigners scattered around the Ministries, but not usually such a concentration of one nationality.

'Owen, I really do feel – '

McKitterick came into the bar, ordered a beer, collected a newspaper from the rack and then went and sat down by himself. Owen gave it a moment or two and then went across.

31

'I read that report,' he said. 'The one your man did on the ghaffirs. You're right. It was a good piece of work.'

'It was, wasn't it?' McKitterick nodded him into the chair opposite. 'Went into everything. We were able to implement it pretty much as it stood.'

'No one asked any questions? Apart from me?'

McKitterick smiled.

'No one. Apart from you.'

'Ah, well. Just goes to show, doesn't it?' He took a sip from his glass. 'You were able to get straight on with it, then?'

'Yes. And just as well we did. This internment thing is hitting us pretty hard.'

'I'm sure. You've had rather a number of posts affected, haven't you?'

'Six'.

McKitterick looked at him.

'Is that another thing that's bothering you?'

'Not any more,' said Owen, smiling amiably.

McKitterick drained his glass.

'Germans are damned efficient,' he said. 'They know what they're doing and they work hard. They've given themselves to this country and worked their guts out for it. And, as far as I'm concerned, that's all there is to it.'

And that, thought Owen, would have been the Khedive's view, too. Desperate to modernize Egypt's creaking medieval systems, he had recruited far and wide, believing that this was the quickest way of gaining access to the technical and management know-how that more developed countries possessed. The result was that his administration was one of the most international in the world, employing experts of almost every nationality, some drawn to Egypt by the lure of higher pay, others simply by the satisfaction of helping to put a developing country on its feet.

For the most part they worked together harmoniously; and now he was extremely angry that a particular group of people in his service should be singled out by the British in this way. They were his servants, not Britain's; and, like

32

McKitterick, as far as he was concerned, if they served him with efficiency and loyalty, that should have been that.

But on this, as on most things, there was little he could do if the British wished it otherwise. Partly in recognition of this, he had just taken himself off in high dudgeon to Constantinople.

In Owen's mail the next day was yet another communication from the Parquet. This time it was a copy of the mamur at Minya's response to the Parquet letter. Clearly taken aback by the speed of the Parquet's reply, and sensing that it implied an importance to the case which he had hitherto not suspected, he had himself responded with unusual celerity.

He listed, as requested, various instances of damage to the walls of the grave, which he attributed to 'Mustapha's foot', and confessed to the disturbance and displacement of sundry feline corpses, which had come about in the course of the removal of the woman's body. Otherwise, God be praised, the site was essentially 'as Pharaoh left it'.

As for the woman herself, the cause of death, according to the hakim, was poisoning by arsenic. After deliberation and much consultation with the husband, the husband's family, and the village at large, the mamur had come to the conclusion that the poison had been self-administered. The woman had always been the odd one out.

The Parquet official had written 'Noted' on the letter and then, in bold, triumphant script: 'Case closed'.

Moved to wrath, Owen wrote back inquiring how, if it was a case of suicide, the mamur could be so confident that the woman had lingered long enough to bandage herself tightly from head to foot, take herself to the grave, and climb in.

Paul rang up to propose a game of tennis.

'It'll have to be singles,' he said, 'now that John and Peter have gone.'

John had left with the regiment a couple of days ago. Peter, who was with another regiment, had gone the week before. Cairo seemed to be emptying.

They met that afternoon, about five, when the heat had gone out of the sun, played a couple of sets and then went to the bar. The bar was almost empty. What people there were at the Gezira were not playing golf or tennis. Owen wondered what they would do for cricket now that the regiments were gone.

'They'll be all right when the Australians come,' said Paul.

'They're definitely coming, are they?'

'Oh, yes. And soon. The Sirdar won't release his regiments until he's sure of replacements. Not with the Turks on the Canal.'

The other side of the Suez Canal was Ottoman ground and for some time there had been rumours of an increasing concentration of troops on that side. Turkey had not yet come into the war and whose side it would come in on was still in doubt. Not that of the British, most people suspected.

Owen told Paul that he had been thinking about his own position.

'They need experienced officers,' he said. 'I've got the experience. It seems wrong not to use it.'

'I've been wondering the same thing,' said Paul. 'Not that I've had your training or experience, of course. Still, I've been wondering whether I ought to volunteer. I've got so far as to think I'll have a word with Kitchener when he gets back.'

'You might have a word with him about me, too.'

'I will. But do you know what I think he's going to say to me? "You're more use here," that's what he'll say.'

He looked at Owen.

'And I think he might say the same of you.'

'I think he might not,' said Owen. 'He doesn't like me.'

'It's not just up to him.'

'Perhaps you could float the idea generally,' said Owen. 'You know, sound people out.'

Paul nodded.

They got up from the table. As they left the verandah, he said:

'Have you talked to Zeinab about it yet?'

*   *   *

34

That was something he'd been deferring; but, as he climbed the stairs to their apartment, he told himself it was something he could not go on putting off. That evening, as they sat over their drinks on the balcony, he broached it.

Zeinab seemed to freeze.

'You can't do that!' she said.

'Well, I know, but –'

'What's the war got to do with you? It's over there. You're here.'

'Well . . .'

'You belong to Egypt now,' she said fiercely. 'You belong to me!'

'Yes, I know, but –'

'What the hell's it got to do with you?' she said again, her eyes filling. 'You've made your life here. With me. Don't I count for anything?'

He tried to put his arm round her, but she shook it off.

'You say one thing and then you do another! You say you love me and then you do – this!'

'Look, I've not done anything yet. And maybe I won't do anything. All I'm doing is thinking about it.'

'Even to think about it,' said Zeinab, 'is wrong. It hurts me. Even for you to think about it!'

She jumped to her feet and ran inside. He heard the door of the bedroom slam.

The telephone was already ringing in the outer office as he went through. Nikos picked it up, listened and then put his hand over the mouthpiece.

'It's another one,' he said.

Owen went on into his office. He heard Nikos say:

'I'll put you through, Effendi.'

He picked up the phone on his desk.

'Yes?'

'Owen, what the hell do you think you're doing? Your men have arrested one of our nurses!'

'Is she German?'

'Her mother's German.'

'Well, then –'

'But her father's English.'

'That ought to be all right, then.'

'But it's not all right! Your men have arrested her.'

'Which Consulate is she registered with?'

Foreign nationals were supposed to register with their Consulate.

'Both.'

'She can't be registered with both. It's got to be one or the other.'

'Why?'

'Well, Christ, you can't be both English and German.'

'What about dual nationality?'

Owen swore quietly to himself.

'Is she registered for dual nationality?' he asked.

'Well, she's registered with both Consulates.'

'But that's not the same thing.'

'Isn't it?'

'No. Look, we're working from a list supplied to the Ministry by the German Consulate and it doesn't say anything about her having dual nationality. What it says is that she's German.'

'Well, she isn't that, is she? Not if she's half English.'

'She ought to have *said* she was half English. Then this wouldn't have happened.'

'I think she just thought . . . All right, all right. The thing is, she can't quite make up her mind which she wants to be. She'd quite like to be both. She says you never know which nationality is going to come in handy.'

'At the moment, it's definitely the British. Look, no matter how she's registered, this is clearly a case of dual nationality – '

'At least.'

'At least?'

'She was born in Egypt. Doesn't that make her Egyptian as well?'

'No. Not unless she wants it.'

'Well, she does want it. Quite. The point is that that's what she is, really. She was born here and has spent all her life here – '

'Look, if she wants to be an Egyptian, she's got to get herself registered as an Egyptian.'

'Yes, but she doesn't want to be just that, she wants to be the others as well. Could she apply for triple nationality, do you think?'

'She's not, by any chance, getting married to a Panamanian?'

Afterwards, though, he fell to wondering about the girl and her situation. It was not uncommon in Egypt. With so many nationalities, it was not surprising if, despite the tensions and barriers between them, sometimes people got married across the lines of division. As, perhaps, he and Zeinab would.

As the girl's parents had. He wondered if they were still alive and, if they were, whether they were living in Egypt. They might well be. In that case the wife might be on one of the lists. Was she being taken away like all the other Germans? The picture came into his mind of the woman on the landing stage at Minya holding out her hands to him. Would it be like that?

It was easy to take people if you thought of them just as names on lists. But Owen had always found it difficult to do that. His mental maps were bristly with the individual reality of people. This was sometimes an advantage to him in his work as Mamur Zapt, sometimes a disadvantage. In the case of taking people into internment it was definitely a disadvantage. Every so often he would become aware of the lives behind the lists and then it was as if a piece of grit had got into the process, like a grain of sand beneath his eyelid, and then he would worry at it and worry at it and be unable to leave it alone.

The woman in the cat cemetery was a bit like that. He had no real sense of her as an individual, yet she refused to go away. Partly it was that the Parquet, with their incompetence, kept bringing her back before him. Partly, though, it was a certain curiosity about the life that lay behind the body; the life of a European married to an Egyptian. How had it gone? he wondered.

*   *   *

37

Yet another communication from the Parquet! Goodness, had they no other work to do? What depth of idiocy would they sink to now? He took the slip of paper out of the envelope and looked at it.

Then he sat up.

The handwriting was different from that of the communications he had recently been receiving. It was small, neat, precise, purposeful.

The message merely said:

I have taken over this case.
Mahmoud

4

Mahmoud el Zaki was one of the Parquet's rising stars and Owen had known him almost ever since he had been in Egypt. He was a young, ambitious lawyer whose ambition, however, took the form less of personal advancement than of advancement for his country. Like the Khedive – a comparison he would have hotly rejected – he wished to free Egypt from the ramshackle practices of the past and see it take a place among the developed nations. Unlike the Khedive, he saw no need for foreign help in achieving this. Egyptians could and should do it on their own. Owen knew exactly where he would stand on the issue of the Germans in the Ministry of the Interior: they shouldn't be there anyway. Egyptians should be doing the work.

Mahmoud felt much the same about Mamur Zapts, too, with this addition, that he didn't believe there should be such a post as Head of the Khedive's Secret Police at all. The Khedive was among the ramshackle practices of the past that he wished to get rid of. Let alone his Secret Police. And as for the post being held by the representative of an occupying power – well, the British were another of the things he wanted to see an end of.

Despite this, he and Owen got on fairly well. Indeed, a slightly surprising friendship had developed between them. They were men of a similar type, cats who walked by themselves; and perhaps the difficulty each found in making close friends among their fellows had made them readier to reach across the British–Egyptian divide.

Owen welcomed his involvement now. At least the case would be properly handled. He picked up his pen and wrote to him, expressing his pleasure and offering his help if needed. He was fairly confident, though, that it would not be drawn upon. On criminal investigation, as on other things, Mahmoud believed that Egypt did not require foreign assistance.

This damned internment business was taking all his time. The lists kept piling up on his desk. He hadn't realized there were so many Germans in Egypt! Come to think of it, he didn't believe there *were* so many. This name, for instance: Abu Ali 'Arrami. That didn't sound very German. Where did he live? Near the Mosque Sayidna Hussein. Right in the middle of the bazaar area. There wasn't a German within miles!

He summoned Nikos.

'This list is a load of old bollocks!' he said. He pointed to the name accusingly.

Nikos looked over his shoulder.

'Not necessarily,' he said. Nikos, Copt bureaucrat that he was, always defended lists. He felt a protectiveness towards them that normal people reserved for their children. 'He might be a German who's converted to the Muslim religion and taken on a Muslim name. Or he might be an Arab who's taken on German nationality, to escape seizure for debt, for instance.'

'Yes, or he might be a sweeper in the Scentmakers' Bazaar who's got a pretty wife whom someone's got his eye on and wants him out of the way!'

'All these things are possible,' Nikos agreed.

'Yes, but do you expect me to waste my time on . . . ?'

Yes, unfortunately; not just Nikos's answer, but that of the dimwits back in London also.

Normally, Owen did the arresting and somebody else did the ferrying to the internment camps. This morning, though, the man in charge of the ferrying was down with malaria and Owen, short-staffed, decided to do the job himself.

There was, too, a particular reason for going with this convoy. It was taking people to the camp to which Fricker,

40

the inspector who had produced the report on the ghaffirs, had been transferred. Owen thought he might have a word with him.

The convoy went first by train and then by cart. They got out of the train at a halt marked only by water tanks and a great arm which swung out over the engine. A line of open carts was drawn up nearby. There followed a long, jolting ride across the desert until suddenly, in the middle of nowhere, Owen saw hundreds and hundreds of tents. When he got closer he saw that they were surrounded by barbed wire.

Soldiers opened a gate in the barbed wire and they drove through. Inside, men laden with pots and pans were queuing up at a stand-by pump for water. They looked at the arrivals curiously and some of them called out greetings.

Owen found Fricker sitting in the entrance to one of the tents, reading a book.

He shrugged.

'No, it is not very nice,' he said. 'But I see the necessity for it. From the British point of view, that is. I have made a list of some suggested improvements. Please be so kind as to give them to the camp commandant when you leave.'

Inside the tent were four *angribs*, native rope beds without mattresses, on two of which men were lying. Beneath each bed was a suitcase, and beside it was a packing case, which served as a bedside table, on top of which some of the men had put personal effects: a set of writing materials, for example. There were remarkably few signs of personal occupation, however. Used to army tents as Owen was, he was struck by how meticulously tidy this one was, and how scant in anything personal; a reflection, he suspected, of Fricker's character.

Fricker went across to the packing case with the writing materials upon it and took out a sheet of paper, which he gave to Owen. It was neatly set out with headings, sub-headings and sub-sub-headings.

Owen folded it and put it in his pocket.

'I was reading a report of yours recently,' he said. 'The one on the ghaffirs. I thought it was good.'

41

Fricker seemed pleased.

'I tried to think of the ghaffirs as a system,' he said. 'It is, I think, the first time that anyone has done that.'

'Yes, the ghaffir has always been seen merely as an individual or as just part of the village.'

'That is so. But if one thinks functionally . . .'

They discussed the report for a while. Then Owen said:

'There is one part, though, that I don't think I go along with you on. Arming the ghaffirs.'

'But they must be armed, if they are to do their duties properly!'

'But need they be armed quite so heavily?'

Fricker shrugged.

'They need to be armed well enough to do the job,' he said.

'The job is usually quite humble. Scaring away the birds, that sort of thing.'

'Usually, but not always. Sometimes they have to fight brigands.'

'Yes, I saw your reference to the situation at Minya.'

'Minya, yes. That is an interesting place.'

'But exceptional, surely? Ghaffirs don't usually have to fight brigands.'

'You have to build it into the system specification, though.'

'Well, do you? I don't think it's fair to expect a ghaffir to fight brigands.'

'Not a ghaffir on his own, no. But that is the point of my report. He should not be asked to fight on his own. When it comes to brigands, he should be operating as part of a group. A trained group, trained for such operations. And with the right weapons to do the job. Superior force, that is the point. At the moment, the ghaffirs do not have superior force. But that is not their fault, it is a fault of the system. And to put that right we have to think of it as a system.'

Owen could see the logic, although he remained unconvinced. He could see, too, why Fricker might appeal to McKitterick. He was analytical, a quality always useful in senior administrators. His mind dwelt too much on the theoretical parameters of his system for Owen's taste, but he could see how it might appeal to others.

What he could not see, however, was any sign that Fricker was playing a deeper game. If anything, his mind seemed to be entirely preoccupied with his work.

Owen asked how he found the Ministry. Was it a congenial place? *Congenial?* Fricker seemed puzzled. 'A good place to work,' amplified Owen, thinking he might not have understood him. 'Oh, yes, most interesting,' said Fricker. Owen decided that it was the concept, not the vocabulary, that was the problem for him.

He asked how Fricker found the Minister. Fricker didn't have much to do with him, not directly. McKitterick? He quite liked McKitterick. He thought he was a very open man. (Open? McKitterick?) But he didn't really have a lot to do with him either. As an inspector, he explained, he worked very much on his own. He was often away touring the provinces. Sometimes he would stay in a place for weeks.

Owen could get no feeling for his private life. He began to suspect he didn't have one. Everything seemed to begin and end in work.

Fricker asked how his colleagues were managing in his absence.

Owen said that they were, of course, below establishment now, which inevitably made a difference.

Fricker shook his head and said that it was very regrettable.

'And unnecessary,' he said. 'For, surely, here in Egypt there is no war. German and Englishman are on the same side. We work together. We are both servants of the Khedive.'

Owen was not without sympathy for this point of view. All the same, it was pretty naïve. And it made it all the more unlikely that Fricker was engaged in the kind of deep plotting that McPhee had supposed. No, Fricker was just an ordinary chap: hard-working, a little narrow, perhaps a bit rigid – even unimaginative.

Which certainly could not be said of McPhee.

*   *   *

'Yes, I know,' said the camp commandant defensively, when Owen gave him Fricker's paper. 'It's not satisfactory. We're working damned hard, but we're not keeping up. That's because you're sending us so many people. At least it's dry, though. When it rains, the place will turn into a morass, and that's when disease will start. I've been in places like this before. In South Africa.

'But it's not because they're prisoners. Go five miles in that direction –' he pointed with his hand – 'and you'll find another camp like this. It, too, is full of people. Only they happen to be soldiers. Our soldiers. That's war for you. Now please get out of my way.'

Zeinab wasn't speaking to him. But she wasn't moving out, either. He took this as a good sign, although he suspected that it merely meant war hadn't been opened on that front yet.

In any case, he still hadn't really made up his mind about volunteering. When he had been with John and the other officers he had been conscious of old fellow-feeling; but now he was remembering that he had left the Army in India precisely because he had thought he didn't have enough fellow-feeling with the officers he met there. Would it be any different in France? Or in Mesopotamia?

But that wasn't really the point, was it?

The war seemed to come closer that lunch-time in the bar of the Sporting Club. Paul was there with two men freshly arrived in Cairo, both of whom Owen knew. One was a man named Cavendish, from the British Embassy in Constantinople, whose role there Owen was not quite sure of but who seemed to feel that he had something in common with Owen.

The other person was a little fair-headed archaeologist, a bit of a know-all, whom Owen hadn't got on with when they had previously met.

'You see,' Cavendish was saying, 'if they play the "holy war" card, it could really cause trouble for us.'

'I don't think it would,' said the archaeologist. 'Not in

44

the Peninsula, at any rate. Tribal rivalries are stronger than religion.'

'How about Egypt, Owen?' said Cavendish, turning towards him.

'Too early to say. In any case, it would be a difficult card to play, wouldn't it? For the Germans.'

'Yes, but not for the Turks.'

'Will they definitely come in?'

'Any day, now. That's why I left Constantinople,' said Cavendish.

'It might be a difficult card even for them. At least, as far as Egypt is concerned. All right, they've got religion in common, but there's as much Nationalist feeling here against the Turks as there is against the British. Almost.'

'If you're really worried about the "holy war" card,' said the little archaeologist, 'you want to get talking to the Sherif.'

'Yes, but he's at Mecca.'

'Go there.'

'I can't,' said Paul. 'Not with Kitchener away.'

'I could,' said the archaeologist.

Both Paul and Cavendish seemed rather taken aback.

'It ought to be someone more senior,' said Cavendish.

'Ought it?' said the archaeologist. 'I could sound him out and then, if he seemed at all responsive, you could send someone more senior.'

Neither Cavendish nor Paul seemed to like the idea.

'We'd better hold it,' said Paul, 'until Kitchener gets back.'

'Is he coming back?'

Paul seemed surprised.

'Well, isn't he?'

'Britain's leading soldier. A war on. They might have something else in mind for him.'

It had never occurred to Owen that Kitchener might not return to Egypt. That would certainly alter things. He had a sudden feeling of elation.

The other three put down their glasses and turned to go, obviously off to some meeting or other.

Cavendish nodded to him.

'We'll be seeing quite a lot of each other,' he said, 'now that

I'm here permanently. We'll probably be setting up some kind of committee, or even a Bureau. I'd like you to be on it.'

'Owen's internal,' said the archaeologist, dissenting.

'That might come in handy,' said Cavendish.

'The war isn't going to be fought in Egypt,' said the archaeologist.

He always rubbed Owen up the wrong way and now something about his tone made Owen take exception.

'There'll be more going on in Egypt than there will be in Mecca,' he retorted.

'Come on, Lawrence,' said Paul impatiently, from the doorway.

He was thinking about it later that afternoon as he drove back over the Kasr-en-Nil Bridge. Below him he could see feluccas shimmering across the water, their graceful lateen sails bowing under the weight of the wind, and at the edge of the river water-sellers wading into the water with their black goatskin bags to fill up for another load.

He asked himself why he took against the man so. They had only met about three times and each time they had rubbed each other up the wrong way.

The first time, Lawrence had made some remark, which Owen had taken to be disparaging, about Owen's ignorance of the world of Oxford colleges that both Lawrence and Paul had once inhabited. Why Owen had taken umbrage at this he couldn't now think. There were plenty of worlds he was on the outside of and usually it didn't bother him.

He decided it must have been the affectation of superiority. Owen didn't take kindly to other people thinking they were superior to him; and Lawrence seemed hardly able to speak without implying that he knew more than the person he was addressing.

He couldn't see them working together on that committee, or Bureau, of Cavendish's. Cavendish himself he didn't exactly warm to, but at least he could get along with him for five minutes without quarrelling. Whereas Lawrence –

And what the hell was the committee all about anyway? It sounded to him like Intelligence work, and he was not sure that he wanted to get involved in that sort of thing. Everything at the moment seemed to be taking him away from his real work. First, all this damned internment stuff, and now, it appeared, Intelligence work of some kind. It was the war, of course. It was affecting everything. He didn't have to go to it. It would come to him, whether he went or stayed, whether he liked it or not.

'And then there's another one,' said the man from the Swiss Consulate, glancing at his list. 'A Mrs Aziz Hanafi.'

'Are you sure she's German?'

The Swiss Consulate had taken over responsibility for looking after the interests of German nationals when the German Consulate had been withdrawn. Problems had come up in the cases of some of the people interned and they were going through them now.

'Yes. Hanafi is her married name. She married an Egyptian. Her original name was Langer. Hilde Langer.'

'Langer?'

The name rang a bell.

'Yes. Actually our concerns here are different from those in the case of the others. This one is deceased.'

'Was she down in Minya?'

'That's right. You know her?'

'I know of her.'

She was the one who had been found in the cat pit.

'Apparently she died in suspicious circumstances.'

'Yes.'

'We don't actually know all the details.'

'I can tell you some of them.'

The man from the Consulate noted them down.

'It's a case of informing the family,' he said. 'Or, rather, of informing our diplomatic colleagues so that they can inform the family.'

He read through the notes.

'It's not very much,' he said. 'I think the family will want to know more.'

'Well, of course, the death is the subject of an investigation.'

'Ye-e-es.'

He sounded doubtful.

'The man in charge of the case now is extremely competent.'

'That's good. Yes, that will help. Do you happen to know his name?'

He wrote it down.

'I'll contact him directly and ask him to keep us informed.'

He hesitated.

'But, you know . . .'

'He really is good, I can assure you.'

'Yes. Yes, I'm sure.' He hesitated again. 'But, you know, these are rather special times, and it would be so easy for things to slip.'

'He won't let them slip, believe me.'

'No, no. Perhaps not.' He hesitated again and then went on resolutely. 'But, you know, in normal times one would have the extra guarantee, in the case of non-Egyptian nationals, that the Mamur Zapt was keeping an eye on things.'

'I'll keep an eye on things, if you want.'

'Yes. Thank you.'

He looked down at his notes. He seemed a decent enough man. This kind of thing was trying and it must be particularly difficult when they weren't even of your own nationality. Owen got up and went to the earthenware jug, covered with a towel, which stood in the window, as in all Cairo offices, and poured him some water. The air coming through the slats of the blinds was supposed to cool the water. He had an uneasy feeling that today the heat was winning. He returned and gave it to the man.

'Thank you.'

He looked down at his notes again and then raised his eyes to Owen resolutely.

'But then there's the other point, you see: her nationality. And you – forgive me – are English.'

'Well . . .'

'Yes, yes, I know. But it would be only natural . . . An enemy, after all . . . war. And you are a busy man, I can see

48

that.' He gestured at the pile of papers on Owen's desk. 'You will have other preoccupations. It would be so easy . . . so easy for this poor woman to fall through the cracks. What is a single person when there is a war on? Especially an unimportant woman. And yet, Captain Owen, it is important. I can say that because I am a neutral. I am outside the war and perhaps I can see things more objectively. It is important *because* she is unimportant. Do you – do you follow me?'

'I follow you.'

'Even during a war. Perhaps especially during a war.'

'I will see that she doesn't fall through the cracks.'

'I will hold you to that. My country – which is not especially fond of Germany – will hold you to that. Will hold England. And Egypt. But above all, Captain Owen, since this is a time when individuals are important, I will hold *you*.'

5

That was all very well, but Mahmoud was actually the one who was conducting the investigation and Owen saw no reason why he should take it over himself. Mahmoud would see it as a personal slight and the strongly Nationalistic Parquet would certainly resist it. Besides, Mahmoud would probably conduct the investigation better than he would. In professional matters, he cut like a knife. This was anyway more Mahmoud's kind of thing than it was Owen's. Owen's experience was on the political side, with the revolutionary 'clubs' and conspiratorial groups with which Cairo abounded, and he didn't imagine that would be of much help in investigating Hilde Langer's death. The murder was much more likely to have been the result of some domestic dispute, he thought, and that was Mahmoud's field, not his.

He wrote to Mahmoud asking to be kept informed, as the Swiss Consulate, acting on behalf of Germany, was taking a particular interest in the matter.

A punctilious note came back from Mahmoud the next day. He would certainly keep Owen informed. Perhaps they could meet when he returned from the visit he would shortly be paying to Minya? Meanwhile, could Owen see what information might be gleaned from the Consulate about the woman's background?

Owen got in touch with the Consulate and the next day he received a couple of sheets of paper: copies from the records which the German Consulate had handed over to them.

Hilde Langer had been born thirty-five years before in a village in West Saxony, that is to say, in Germany not Egypt.

Her father had been pastor of the local church. Her mother had died three years after she was born, giving birth to another daughter, who had, alas, not survived her. The father, considerably older than the mother, had himself died not long after, and relatives had sent the small girl to her mother's sister in Alexandria.

The girl had grown up in Alexandria, where her uncle was an exporter of tobacco, but then, when she was eighteen, the family had moved to Cairo.

Only two years later the uncle had been severely incapacitated by a stroke and the aunt had sold the business and taken him back to Germany. Hilde Langer, however, had not returned with them.

What she had done then was not clear. There was a gap of five years and then the next item recorded was the date of her marriage to an Egyptian national, a Mr Aziz Hanafi.

Shortly after this there was a note of a change of residence to an address in Assuan. The couple appeared to have remained there for two years and then there was a brief indication that the registree had left the country. The final item, dated four years later, was a note of re-registration on return to the country. The address this time was the sugar factory down in Minya.

About the only thing that could be gleaned about the latter years, thought Owen, was that she had been meticulous in her registrations.

He wondered where the information had come from about her earlier years.

'I don't know,' said the man at the Consulate, 'or why the Germans had it on record. But I know someone you can ask about the time at Alexandria. It's an old lady who knew the family quite well.'

'Are you sure she's still around?'

'She's not German, if that's what you're saying,' said the man, with a touch of acerbity. 'She's registered with us.'

'Swiss?'

'Yes. She's quite old now and we've been keeping an eye on her. One of us goes down twice a year. In fact, it's quite

51

a treat. She's a mine of information on the old expatriate communities.'

Owen took her name.

'If I were you, I'd write,' said the man. 'She likes to take her time these days, and she's one of that generation that writes good letters.'

'What about the Cairo years? They're actually the ones that are likely to be most relevant.'

'Can't help you there, I'm afraid. It was before I came here. Wait a minute, I'll ask Müller.'

Another voice came on the line.

'Müller here. How can I help?'

'Owen, the Mamur Zapt.'

'The Mamur Zapt?'

'Yes. I'm looking for information on a Hilde Langer, who would have been in Cairo, oh, ten to fifteen years ago.'

'Langer? I'm sorry, I don't remember anyone . . .'

'She would have been in her early twenties.'

'It sounds as if I ought to have known her. Was she pretty?'

'Hard to tell.' He thought back to the face in the cat cemetery. 'Fair, anyway.'

'They're all fair. At least in memory. Anything else you can tell me?'

Owen looked at his papers again.

'She came here from Alexandria with an uncle and aunt. The uncle was a tobacco exporter. Knipper, his name was.'

'I remember the Knippers. But the niece . . . I really ought to. If she was with the Knippers. The Swiss community here was very small in those days.'

'She was German.'

'We would have met. All the German speakers. We liked the chance to speak German. Otherwise it was Arabic all the time, or French, or English. There were things every week. Parties, musical evenings, that sort of thing. Cards. Any excuse to get together. So I should have met her. Especially if she was young. I was just out from Switzerland, an unattached male, nostalgic for home beauty . . . But I don't remember her at all. Odd, isn't it?'

'You don't know anyone else who might remember those days?'

'The Kleins, the Grünmanns. The Spitzers, perhaps ... Wait a minute, was she at all musical?'

'She might have been,' said Owen, remembering the piano. 'She might well have been.'

'Well, look, as a last resort you could try Puttendorf. But God knows what state he's in nowadays.'

'Where will I find him?'

'In a bar, certainly. Try Fritz's, just off the Ezbekiya. Most evenings. And afternoons and mornings for that matter.'

'Lunch-times?' said Owen.

'Especially. Offer to take him to the Continentale for a drink. He'll like that. It'll remind him of old times.'

'Look, thanks very much. I hadn't realized the Swiss–German connection would be so helpful.'

'Just don't confuse the two, please. Especially at the moment.'

The Kleins lived in a tall house just off the Midan Nasriya. They were obviously well-to-do. A suffragi opened the door and led Owen to an upstairs sitting room, where the Kleins were having afternoon tea. They were an elderly couple, rather frail now, but still mentally alert. They remembered the Knippers very well. But the niece?

'Are you sure?' said Mrs Klein doubtfully. 'I don't remember a niece.'

'I remember a girl, I think,' said Mr Klein.

'You always remember a girl,' said his wife, somewhat tartly.

'But was her name Hilde?'

'Eva, I think,' said Mrs Klein.

'Perhaps it was.'

'But a Hilde Langer . . .'

Mrs Klein shook her head.

It was a similar story at the Grünmanns, where he was offered some cherry brandy and a thick slab of caraway seed cake covered with cream. Owen hadn't tasted cream for some time. You tended to fight shy of milk products, both in Egypt and in India. It took him back to his childhood in a Welsh parsonage, and he had some more.

It was very agreeable and so were the Grünmanns; but on Hilde Langer he again drew a blank.

'In her twenties? Well, there wouldn't have been many girls in their twenties, not out here all the time. Are you sure she didn't come out just for the season?'

'No, she was with her uncle and aunt. They moved here from Alexandria.'

'I remember the Knippers,' said Mr Grünmann. 'He was in tobacco, wasn't he?'

'It was such a shock,' said Mrs Grünmann. 'I felt so much for Rumi Knipper.'

'She was quite right to take him home. The heat out here . . . for a sick man . . .'

'The niece didn't go back with them. She stayed out here.'

'I really don't remember,' said Mrs Grünmann, looking at her husband. 'Do you?'

'What was her name, again?'

It was strange, thought Owen, how they recreated their homes in the style to which they had been accustomed. He had never had much to do with either the Swiss or the German expatriate communities and wasn't aware of ever having entered their houses, but the houses he had visited today had had things in common and he was sure that was a reflection of styles back at home. Wood was very much in evidence, for example, in the furniture, the knick-knacks, even the eating utensils. The styles were inclined to the heavy – there was a world of difference between them and those he had seen in the houses of French expatriates. Certainly you would never have thought you were in Egypt.

The Spitzers were younger than the Kleins and the Grünmanns.

'Did she play tennis?' asked Mrs Spitzer.

'I'm sorry, I –'

'I don't think she could have,' said Mr Spitzer. 'Otherwise we'd have remembered her.'

'Do you remember the Knippers?'

'Oh, yes. I felt so sorry for them. It came as a complete shock.'

'But there wasn't much else they could do, was there?'

'It was best to go home,' said Mrs Spitzer firmly.

'She was a young woman, fair-haired –'

'She has disappeared from my mind completely,' said Mrs Spitzer. 'If she was ever there.'

'Mine, too,' said Mr Spitzer.

She had disappeared from everyone's mind completely, thought Owen, as he walked home. So completely as to make him wonder, too, if she had ever been there. But there was the name in the Consulate files and the meticulous registrations. There was also, indubitably, the body in the cat cemetery.

And there was something odd about this. They all remembered the Knippers very clearly, yet the Knippers, by his count, had been in Cairo for not much more than two years. Whereas Hilde Langer had been there for seven.

If, of course, she had been there. Perhaps she had merely registered in Cairo and then gone somewhere else. But where, in Egypt, could a solitary, unattached, young European woman go? What could she do? Not a job, in this most male-dominated of countries, certainly. How would she have lived? On an allowance made her by the Knippers? But even then, how in a place like Egypt, would she have been able to manage on her own?

Had she been on her own, though? What about her husband? He had seemingly only come into the picture five years later. Or had they been living together before the marriage?

But, Christ, an Egyptian and a European? Hell, he and Zeinab were conscious of the pressures even now. How had it been then?

Of course, she could simply have returned to Alexandria, where there might have been friends, or family, to support her. He would have to write that letter to the old lady the man from the Consulate had mentioned.

And meanwhile, perhaps, he could try that evidently rather dubious character Müller had told him about. What was his name? Puttendorf. He would try him tomorrow, at lunch-time. Before he had soaked up so much alcohol as to be completely incapable of responding coherently.

Fritz's was in the Wagh-el-Birket, just off the Ezbekiya Gardens.

Owen liked the Ezbekiya Gardens. He liked the donkey-boys squatting round the large trays in the pavement cafés, dipping their fingers into the meat dishes and helping themselves to the bread stuck on the spikes round the rim; he liked the camel men spreading green fodder all over the road for their camels, the Nubians sprawled on the pavement with mandarin oranges piled like cannonballs before them. He liked the chestnut sellers roasting chestnuts over the gratings round the young trees, the peanut and dried-bean sellers, the men who sold cups of hot sago.

He liked the people who made shops out of the railings that ran round the Gardens, twining whips and ribbons and dirty postcards through the ironwork; he liked the leaning, Pisa-like towers of tarbushes piled on top of each other; the barber perching on the railings while he cut the hair of the man squatting on the pavement below; he liked even the sweet sellers, with their fly-speckled trays of caramel and Turkish delight and their big cheeses of nougat.

But he did not like the Wagh-el-Birket, equally picturesque though it was, in its way. On one side was an arcade with dubious cafés under its arches, where from the tables outside the customers could view the houses opposite with their balconied upper floors from which, later, the ladies of the night would lean out in their flimsy robes, illuminated by the rose light of the lanterns behind them.

At this hour of day the balconies were deserted, the curtains drawn. The few customers at the tables across the street could gaze only at the extremely large, heavily hennaed ladies of the less expensive lower floors, smiling indefatigably from the open windows.

Fritz's was at the far end of the street, just before the café with the female band (not strong musically, perhaps, but rumoured to be highly competent in other ways). As the cafés under the arches went, Fritz's was not too bad a place. The floor was fairly clean and a one-eyed Arab was mopping the stone tops of the tables. In one corner of the room was a piano, at which a man was sitting.

He was not playing – indeed, just at the moment he seemed hardly in a condition to – but from time to time one hand would touch, almost caress, the keys. But then it would immediately move to the glass standing on the end of the keyboard.

There was a traditional European-style bar and a man behind it who may even have been Fritz, since he wore Bavarian braces.

'Puttendorf?' said Owen, jerking his head in the direction of the man at the piano.

The bartender nodded.

The man at the piano swivelled round.

'Who asks for Puttendorf?'

Owen went across to him.

'I do,' he said.

Puttendorf tried to look at him but his eyes refused to focus. After a moment he turned back to the piano and said: 'No one asks for Puttendorf.'

Owen turned him round.

'Puttendorf,' he said, 'I want to talk to you.'

Puttendorf shook his head.

'No one wants to talk to Puttendorf. Not these days.'

He collapsed back over the piano in tears.

Owen looked at the bartender.

'Is there a better time?'

'To speak to him? No.'

Owen considered.

'If I take him outside,' he asked, 'will he fall over?'

'Oh, no,' said the bartender confidently, 'not for some hours yet.'

Owen bent down.

'Puttendorf,' he said, shaking him gently, 'I want to have a talk. Let's go somewhere else. How about the Continentale?'

Puttendorf straightened up.

'The Continentale?' he said. 'I was just on my way there.' He tried to look at his watch. 'Goodness me, I should have been there already. Fritz, why didn't you tell me?'

He tried to stand up. Owen helped him.

'He'll be all right now,' said Fritz.

Amazingly, once he was outside he seemed to recover; enough, at any rate, to walk the comparatively short distance along the south side of the Garden to the Hotel Continentale.

Once inside, he sniffed the air appreciatively. It was cool from the great fans hissing overhead and carried faint aromas from the dining room of bouillon and coffee. Owen led him to a corner of the bar and they sat down.

'Of course, they all know me here,' said Puttendorf.

He waved to the waiters.

'Hello, François! Abdul!'

François came across.

'Hello, Mr Puttendorf! You're still keeping well, I see. What can I get you?'

'Two beers, please,' said Owen.

François came back with the beers and set them down.

'He's only allowed the one,' he whispered to Owen.

Puttendorf was looking puzzled.

'Why aren't they playing, François?'

'They're taking a break. In a moment you'll hear them tuning up.'

'Ah, good.' Puttendorf seemed relieved. 'I used to play here, you know,' he said to Owen.

'With the orchestra?'

'Yes.' He looked at his hands. 'Not any more, though.' He showed them to Owen. They shook continuously.

Puttendorf laughed.

'They used to say that everything was vibrato with me! But that was only at the end.'

'You were in the strings?'

'Violins. I played first at one time, when I had just come out here.'

'How long ago was that?'

'Let me see . . .' The eyes clouded, then cleared again. 'I

58

don't remember,' he said. 'Twenty . . . thirty? Was it thirty years ago?'

'A long time, anyway. Actually, I wanted to ask you something about that. Did you ever know a woman called Hilde Langer?'

'What did she play?'

'The piano, I think. But she may have played something else.'

'No, the piano. That was the problem, you see. You can't earn a living with the piano. Not unless you teach. Well, she did do some of that, as we all did. But she wanted to do more. She wanted to become a concert pianist. "Hilde," I said, "we all fancy ourselves as concert musicians. But only a few of us ever make it. And that is especially true if you play the piano. What happens if you don't make it? There is nothing to fall back upon. With other instruments you can always try for an orchestra." "The trouble is," she said, "my nature is that of a soloist."

'Of course, she didn't get anywhere. A few concerts, perhaps, at the houses of friends. But even then it was mostly as an accompanist. She had a real talent for that, I will say. Especially for Lieder. We used to sing a lot of Lieder in those days. People would take it in turns to host an evening. It wasn't always music. Sometimes it was cards. Or those dreadful charades. There was usually something every week. The German-speaking community was quite a small one then, and I suppose we felt the need. You know, in a foreign country. You keep together more, don't you?

'And I suppose to sing Lieder reminded us of home. They were German, weren't they? Peculiarly German. Not like cards.

'So for a time she did quite well. It was always, "Hilde, darling, you will play for us, won't you?" They used to pay her, of course. They knew how things stood. "Hilde, dear, you're a professional, after all, and we know professionals don't do things for nothing. So . . ." And she would smile prettily and say, "Well, I'm only a *little* professional." And they would say: "It's only a little money," and everyone would laugh.

59

'But she *had* to be professional. There was a tenor, I remember, who was very popular for a while and who was always being invited to sing at evenings. He liked her to accompany him. And he would stand at the piano looking down soulfully at her, and she would sit looking up at him with her great round eyes, and it was all very romantic, and people loved it. They thought it was really like that, that he and she . . .

'But of course it wasn't. She was just being professional. She knew that was what they wanted and she gave it them. But when it turned out not to be like that, I think they felt disappointed. They felt cheated. And, do you know, I think it could have been a contributory factor to them turning against her. They felt let down. Then, of course, when she . . . It made it so much worse.'

He looked down at his glass.

'Do you think I could have another one?'

'They won't let you.'

'Give me yours and get another one. They'll let *you*.'

He took Owen's half-empty glass and poured what was left into his own.

'When she . . . ?' prompted Owen.

Puttendorf looked at him blankly.

'Why did they turn against her?'

Puttendorf made an effort to continue but Owen saw it slipping away from him.

'Why did people turn against Hilde Langer?'

Puttendorf tried again but failed.

'It was good then,' he said, his mind beginning to wander. 'People cared for each other.' He began to weep. 'No one cares for Puttendorf,' he said. 'Not any more.'

'They do. You just don't see it.'

'Only God cares for Puttendorf. And do you know why? Because Puttendorf is dead.'

Owen left him weeping silently and went up to the bar.

'Where does he usually go next?'

'Fritz's?'

'He's just come from there.'

'Simoun's?'

60

'Where's that?'

'Round the corner from Fritz's.'

'I'll take him there.'

They went this time through the Gardens. Owen thought he remembered fountains there. If not, there was the lake.

They found a fountain just inside the gate and Owen made Puttendorf duck his head into the bowl. It seemed to revive him, and as they walked on through the baobabs and papayas he looked around appreciatively.

'I used to come here,' he said.

'Don't you still?'

Puttendorf shook his head. It cost a piastre to come in.

They went past the bandstand.

'Wind,' said Puttendorf disapprovingly. 'Wind, and percussion. That's all.'

A native band was playing there. There was the wail of bagpipes.

'What is the line between the barbarians and the romantic?' asked Puttendorf. 'I find the native bagpipes barbarous. But the same bagpipes, played by the Scots, are romantic.'

'Was Hilde Langer romantic?'

'She must have been. Otherwise why did she go off with that Egyptian?'

He stole a glance at Owen.

'Or perhaps she was just being barbaric.'

'What did people think?'

Puttendorf was silent for so long that Owen thought his mind had gone wandering again. It hadn't though; he was thinking.

'They were shocked. At first they couldn't believe it. Not that nice Hilde Langer. But then, she had always been a little odd, hadn't she? Staying on here alone when she could have gone back. And after the Knippers had been so good to her! Like a father and mother. And then, just when she might have repaid some of that care and love, she goes off on her own and tries to become a pianist! That is unfeeling. Worse than that; it is not normal.'

Puttendorf laughed to himself.

'Hah, it is not normal to become a musician and the little

burghers of Cairo feel uncomfortable. They do not like it. But they would not have found that out if it had not been for the Egyptian. That made them see her in a new light, the true light. There are degrees of oddity, yes, and to be a musician, well, that is at the very limit of acceptability. But to marry an Egyptian, that is to go beyond the limit. And so it was out, out for our dear little Hilde. Out, out into the darkness.'

6

Mahmoud came threading his way through the tables towards him. At every table someone jumped up and shook his hand. It was the custom in Egypt and yet Owen was a little surprised. He had not suspected that Mahmoud had so many acquaintances. He had always seemed a very solitary man. He spotted Owen and waved a hand, but then someone folded him in a deep embrace. It took him some time to work his way across the café.

At this hour, the hour when Cairo came alive again after its siesta, the tables were all full. The young office workers, who, only a few hours before had streamed exhausted from the huge office blocks around the square, from the Credit Lyonnais, the Tribunaux, the Poste and the Dette, had returned, revived, to make the most of the evening. There was an atmosphere of conviviality, almost of gaiety.

Mahmoud at last arrived. He threw his arms round Owen.

'So long!' he cried. 'So long since I have seen you!'

'Too long! See what comes of getting married!' Mahmoud had married shortly before. 'How is Aisha?'

'Well. And Zeinab?'

'Well, too.'

He told Mahmoud about the move into the shared apartment. He had been afraid that the strait-laced Mahmoud might disapprove, but he seemed genuinely pleased.

'That is good,' he said approvingly. 'It is best for a man. Or so I have found.'

He laughed, a trifle self-consciously. Owen thought he had changed, in even a few weeks. He seemed more confident, more relaxed, less intense. Happier?

63

'You too,' he said, laying his hand affectionately on Owen's arm in the Arab fashion. 'With Zeinab.'

'Thinking about it,' said Owen.

Mahmoud dropped into the chair opposite.

'But you must not blame Aisha,' he said. 'The fact is, I have just taken up a new job.'

'Promotion, I hope?'

'Well . . . Let's say I tell others what to do now instead of doing it myself. Which usually means that it's done less well and so I have to do it again myself.'

Owen could imagine that. Mahmoud set high standards for himself and was astonished when other people did not do likewise. It was not just a matter of personal morality but was bound up with his intense nationalism. He could not bear Egypt to fall short.

'And so you work late, I suppose?' he said. 'Much to Aisha's annoyance, I imagine.'

'"Mahmoud," she says, "why cannot you be like other men?" My mother, she also says that.'

As was the custom in Egypt, they lived with his mother.

'But then,' said Mahmoud, 'she always has!'

They both laughed. Yes, thought Owen, he had changed. In the past he would never have been able to laugh at himself. It must be Aisha's doing. He felt a twinge of – what was it? Nostalgia? Envy?

'It is good to see you,' he said.

'And you too. I have been meaning to invite you round, but somehow have always been too busy. So it is good that we have been brought together.'

'The woman at Minya?'

Mahmoud nodded.

'I owe you an apology,' he said soberly. 'The Parquet owes you an apology.'

'No, really – '

'We do. The case has been very badly handled. Very badly. I saw that as soon as I looked at it. I feel ashamed. I have spoken to the people concerned.'

'Not on my account, please.'

'No, not on your account.'

64

Mahmoud was silent. Owen knew exactly what he was thinking. It was another example of Egypt falling short. Sometimes Mahmoud despaired.

'It is not themselves they have let down,' he said darkly. 'It is Egypt.'

'I have spoken to the Swiss Consulate,' Owen said. 'I told them that the case was in good hands.'

'I have spoken to them too,' said Mahmoud, 'since I got back from Minya. They did not seem too sure.'

'It's not just you,' said Owen. He told him about the exchange with the Consulate man. 'He was concerned, I think, that, what with the war, and her being a German, she might fall through the cracks.'

'Fall through the cracks?' The phrase was new to Mahmoud. He tasted it and quite liked it. 'No,' he said, 'he is right. We must see that she doesn't fall through the cracks.'

'Tell me about Minya,' said Owen.

How many people there were in the house, he had never quite succeeded in working out. There were children, certainly, a lot of children, and they belonged to several different families. There were brothers, perhaps three of them, their wives, presumably, and their mother. But then there seemed to be others. Sisters? Sisters' husbands? He was never quite sure.

For a start, he couldn't quite see them because in the house it was so dark. There didn't seem to be any windows. And then they couldn't all get in the room. He could hear people moving about in other rooms and there were certainly people listening in the doorway. It was like addressing a village meeting.

And then for the most part only the men spoke.

He asked them how long they had been in the house.

'Two years,' said one of the men.

'We came when Aziz came,' said another of the brothers.

'You work in the fields?'

'In the fields!' said the first brother indignantly. 'What do you think we are?'

'Do you think we're fellahin or something?'

'Where do you work, then?'

'At the factory. Sometimes.'

'Loading cane?'

'It's busy now,' said some evasively.

But not busy at other times, thought Mahmoud. Most times.

'There are many of you,' he said.

'God has been bountiful.'

'My family has always been fruitful,' said a woman's voice determinedly. The grandmother, presumably.

'Who does the cooking?' asked Mahmoud.

'All of us.'

'You can't expect me to,' said the grandmother, 'not when I've got four daughters-in-law in the house.'

'We take it in turns,' said another woman.

'And prepare the food together?'

'Usually.'

'The foreign woman too?'

'Yes.'

There seemed some dissent.

'Sometimes.'

'She kills the food,' said another voice.

There was general agreement about that.

'Useless!' said the grandmother. 'Can't cut up, can't cook, can't have children, can't do anything!'

'She does her share!' objected a younger voice.

'Speak when you're spoken to, Fatima!' said a man's voice.

Mahmoud decided to have a private word with Fatima.

'But then she feeds it to the cats!' said someone.

'No wonder she came and got her!' said someone spitefully.

'What?' said Mahmoud.

'The Cat Woman. That's what happened in the end. The Cat Woman came and got her. And good riddance, too!'

'What woman is this?'

'The Cat Woman. She lives in the cane.'

'She jumped over the wall,' said someone.

'You saw this?' said Mahmoud sceptically.

'No, but I saw the footmarks.'

'I heard the thud,' said another man, 'and went out.'

'And did you see her?'

'No, but that was because she had jumped back again.'

Mahmoud decided that the session was disintegrating and sent them all out.

Then he had gone in to see the husband. He had found him, as Owen had, lying on a bed in a darkened room, so dark that Mahmoud couldn't see the expression on his face, something he never liked when he was questioning people but which on this occasion he put up with out of respect for the man's grief.

Aziz Hanafi answered his question almost inaudibly.

Mahmoud said that the news must have come as a terrible shock to him. Hanafi inclined his head slightly. Mahmoud asked when it was that he had first heard. Soon after the body had been found, he said. The omda had come straight to him.

And that was?

In the morning. About mid-way through the morning. Men working nearby had seen that a grave had been disturbed and had told the omda, the village headman. The omda had fetched the mamur and together they had unwrapped the bandage. And then the omda had come and told him.

'Were you surprised?'

Surprised? He had lifted his head.

'Had you feared that something like this might have happened?'

'No. How could I have feared? Something like this . . . It is not to be thought of.'

'Not exactly like this, perhaps. But did you not fear that something bad might have happened to her?'

'No. Not like this.'

'Had you not feared, when you came home from your work at the factory, and found her not there?'

'Not at first. I thought she had gone to the market.'

'But then, as time passed?'

'Then I feared, yes. But it was not . . . not this that I feared.'

'What was it that you feared?'

'That she had left me.'

The words were almost inaudible.

'She had talked of that?'

'No. Never.'

'But you guessed, perhaps, that she had thought of that?'

'She was troubled, I knew that.'

'About the marriage?'

'It had never been easy. And now it was getting even harder.'

'Why was that?'

'It was a mistake coming here!' the man broke out. 'If we had gone to the city there would have been others . . . others she could have talked to. Here . . . there were only my people.'

'Your family?'

'We could not go to them. They came to us.'

'You were the one with the job?'

'I had responsibilities to them. She could never understand that. I said: "It is our way – to care for our people." She said: "Your mother, I can understand. But everybody?" I said: "I am the one that God has blessed, and therefore I must see to the others of my family."'

'You quarrelled about this?'

'Quarrelled? No, not quarrelled. We never quarrelled, not even with all the hard things that have happened to us.' His voice broke. 'She was an angel of light,' he said. 'She was my all.'

'But you knew she was unhappy. And so, when she did not come home, you began to fear?'

'I began to fear, yes. But not this!' Mahmoud could see him beginning to shake. 'Not this!'

On the way out he met the doctor, Mr Kufti.

'You had better go to him,' Mahmoud said.

Kufti nodded.

'I will give him a sedative,' he said.

Mahmoud waited until he came out.

'I have read your report,' he said.

'Yes?'

'A very helpful one. There is one thing, though, that I wish you could clarify for me. You are confident about the cause of death?'

'Arsenic,' said the doctor. 'There was no sign of an external injury.'

'Quite so. But are you able to tell me whether the arsenic was taken in one large dose or in several doses?'

The doctor smiled.

'The former being more consistent with self-administration. Suicide or . . . ?'

'Exactly.'

'I am afraid not. Perhaps your laboratories in Cairo will be able to be more precise.'

'I don't know that we could get the body up there now. Or whether it would be worth it. There is another question, though, that I would like to ask which is related. Can you give me any indication of when approximately the poison was ingested?'

'As you say, the answer relates to your former question. I am unable to be specific. Within the forty-eight hours prior to her death, certainly. But whether . . . If you pressed me,' said Mr Kufti reluctantly, 'I would say that the symptoms are consistent with it being administered in several doses over two or three days.'

'Thank you,' said Mahmoud.

Before leaving the house, Mahmoud had summoned Fatima, the dissentient voice in the general meeting with the family. When she appeared, a man was with her. This was normal. In Egypt a stranger might not address a married woman directly. Any remarks or questions had to be put to her through a male relative, usually her husband, and this was adhered to even in the case of a police investigation. It was, therefore, the man whom Mahmoud had addressed.

'I wish to ask,' he said, 'about the preparation of meals in the household in the days immediately before Mrs Hanafi's death.'

'She doesn't know anything about it,' said the man.

'And in particular,' pursued Mahmoud, 'the extent to which Mrs Hanafi herself was involved in the preparation.'

'She hasn't got anything to say,' said the man.

'Oh, but I think she has,' said Mahmoud, looking now directly at the woman. 'For did she not say, when we were all together just now, that Mrs Hanafi assisted sometimes in the preparation?'

'I certainly did,' said the woman.

'Fatima, you shut up!' said the man.

Fatima turned to him.

'I said it, didn't I? And it's true. So why should I deny it?'

'Fatima, one word more from you and I shall give you a good beating!'

'Beat her,' said Mahmoud, 'and I shall beat you!'

'But I'm her husband.'

'He won't beat me,' said the woman calmly. 'He's too afraid to. He knows I carry a knife under my burka.'

'Fatima!'

'Go on, ask me,' said Fatima, turning to Mahmoud.

'Fatima, I will not allow –'

'Out!' said Mahmoud.

'Out?' said the man, astounded.

'Out!'

The man shuffled towards the door and then stopped uncertainly.

'But –'

Mahmoud grabbed him by the shoulder, pushed him through the door and then closed the door behind him.

'He'll stay there listening,' said Fatima.

Mahmoud opened the door, seized the man and pushed him along the corridor.

'Away!' he said. 'Or else there'll be trouble!'

The man slunk away. Mahmoud closed the door and came back into the room. He was surprised at himself, slightly shocked. He was normally punctilious in his observance of the forms, especially when it came to women. How had this happened?

Fatima smiled with satisfaction.

70

'Why didn't you take a stick to him?' she said. 'It would have done him good.'

Mahmoud pulled himself together.

'Fatima,' he said severely, 'a bad thing has been done. God sees all, and therefore you must tell me. Do you know how she died?'

'No. God is my witness, no.'

'It was not an agreed thing?'

'In this family,' said Fatima, 'nothing is agreed.'

'The foreign woman was not liked?'

'I did not mind her. She was nice to me when Abu was born.'

'Could something have been put in her food?'

Fatima considered.

'It would have been hard,' she said. 'We all eat out of one pot.'

She considered some more.

'However,' she said, 'it could have been done. For although she took her food out of the common pot, she did not always eat with us. Sometimes she took a bowl outside, saying she would eat it where there was more air. It was then that she would give it to the cat.'

'So perhaps when she took it out, someone could have put something in?'

'That is so. But it would not have been easy, for she would have taken her bowl with her and kept it in her hand.'

Mahmoud nodded.

'Fatima,' he said, 'had she been at all unwell?'

'She was always complaining of the heat.'

'Had she complained of stomach pains? Sickness of the stomach?'

'Hah!' said Fatima. 'What a to-do there would have been if she had! They would have thought a child was coming.'

'What a house!' said Mrs Schneider with a shudder. 'What a family! It seemed to swallow her up. You never really saw her. You only caught glimpses of her. And when you did she always seemed so lifeless. As if they had sucked all the blood out of her. She was like a ghost. I had seen her once or twice at the beginning and then she seemed so ... so bubbly, almost. So ... excited. And then I didn't see her for some time. When I did see her again there was no ... no animation about her at all. The only time she came to life, I think, was when she was playing the piano.'

'She used to play often?'

'Oh, for hours and hours.'

'Got on my nerves,' said Mr Schneider.

'I didn't use to mind it,' said Mrs Schneider, 'but it must have been difficult for the other people in the house.'

'Did you ever call on her?'

'No ...' Mrs Schneider hesitated. 'It wasn't ... wasn't easy.'

'It's not a thing you do,' said Mr Schneider. 'I mean, I see a lot of Hanafi at work, and get on with him very well. He's an intelligent, hard-working chap. A bit quiet, perhaps. But we've always got along well. I daresay if he'd been European we would have met socially. You know, have them along for a drink, or to play cards. But somehow you can't really do that if they're Egyptian. They don't drink, for a start. Probably don't play cards. And then – well, it's just not done in Egypt, is it? You never see the women. Do you ever meet your colleagues' wives, Mr Zaki?'

'No,' Mahmoud had to confess.

'You meet them, though, probably. But not their wives.'

'I feel sorry now,' said Mrs Schneider.

'You see, it was awkward. We didn't know whether to treat her as an Egyptian or as a European.'

'I could have called on her, I suppose,' said Mrs Schneider. 'But, somehow, that family –!'

'Hundreds of them!' said Mr Schneider. 'God knows what it was like in that house.'

'I thought it might make things worse,' said Mrs Schneider. 'We knew they didn't get on very well.'

'Did anyone call on them?' asked Mahmoud. 'Did she have any friends?'

'There was a Greek family over in Minya. She used to give the children piano lessons. Otherwise –'

'There was that man,' said Mr Schneider.

'What man was this?' asked Mahmoud.

'He was based down here for a while. Looking into the ghaffirs. Anyway, he and Hanafi struck up an acquaintance and Hanafi invited him over to his house. And then, do you know what? You'll never believe this.'

'No?'

'He used to sing.'

'Sing? While he was in the house?'

'She used to play for him,' said Mrs Schneider.

'Sing! That must have gone down like a bomb with the rest of the Hanafis.'

'They weren't alone. Her husband was there.'

'Yes, I know, but – sing!'

'He sang very beautifully,' said Mrs Schneider. 'And she played very beautifully, too.'

'Yes, but, look, that might be all right in Cairo – though I don't know how it would go down even there! What would your people think, Mr Zaki, if you brought home some bloke and he settled down to singing with your wife?'

Mahmoud had strong words for the mamur when at last he succeeded in cornering him.

'What nonsense is this? She took enough poison to kill herself, bandaged herself from toe to head like a mummy, walked half a mile and then put herself into a grave: is that what you are saying? Suicide? You foolish man!'

But the mamur was, perhaps, not quite so foolish.

'There are two things,' he said. 'The manner of the dying, and the body. As to the manner, who can tell? God alone sees all. But as to the body, that is a different matter. A body causes trouble. Especially if it is the body of a foreigner. The omda comes, the mamur comes, the Parquet come. Even the Mamur Zapt comes! So what do you do if you are so unfortunate as to find one? You get rid of it.'

'You could tell the omda.'

'But then would come the questions.'

'Why not just leave it alone?'

'But then they would ask you why you had not told the omda!'

'Are you suggesting that somebody might just have come upon the body by accident and decided to get rid of it?'

'That is right, yes.'

'Without pausing to ask how the person died?'

'Well . . .'

'Even if that were so, you, the mamur, should ask how the person died.'

'I did! I talked to everyone. And we all agreed: she had committed suicide.'

'How could you be so sure?'

'Well, it stands to reason, doesn't it? She was a foreigner.'

'What's that got to do with it?'

'A foreign *woman*,' emphasized the mamur.

'Well?'

'They don't fit in.'

'If they are taken into a family, they become part of the family.'

'Well,' said the mamur. 'Up to a point.'

'Why should she not fit in?'

The mamur looked at his feet.

'There was no son,' he said, after a moment.

'So?'

'It stands to reason that she would feel ashamed.'

'You think she killed herself because of that?'

'Best thing,' said the mamur.

'There are things to be done,' said Mahmoud.

The mamur looked depressed.

'First, where do you buy arsenic round here?'

'Arsenic?' said the mamur, affecting shock. 'You don't buy it.'

'Oh, yes, you do,' said Mahmoud.

The fact was that poisoning your neighbour's buffalo was something of a traditional sport in Egyptian villages.

'Is there someone in the village?'

'I really couldn't say –' began the mamur.

'Then find out,' said Mahmoud. 'And ask if the woman went there.'

'These foreigners –'

'Might not know the ways of the village, and so she might have gone to a shop in Minya. Ask there, too. And, finally . . .'

'Yes, Effendi?' said the mamur, unenthusiastically.

'The bandages that were used to bind the woman: where did they come from? The hospital? The hakim? A shop? There were a lot of them. Someone will remember.'

Finally, Mahmoud had gone to see the village omda. After going through with him his part in the proceedings, he had said:

'Death, I can understand. Hiding the body, I can understand. But to hide it in such a manner and such a place, that I cannot understand. Can you, as a man wise in the ways of the sugar cane people, tell me why that might have been so?'

'They do say,' said the omda cautiously, 'that she was taken by the Cat Woman.'

'The Hanafis say that,' said Mahmoud, 'but that is mere foolishness.'

'Well . . .' said the omda.

'Surely, you, an omda and a man of wisdom, do not believe such nonsense?'

'Well . . .'

'Cat Woman! That is the stuff of old women's tales!' said Mahmoud scornfully.

'Well . . .'

'It is a thing of fancy – fancy and superstition. There never was such a thing.'

'Yes, but –'

'Tell me: have you, has anyone, ever seen such a creature?'

'Abdul has.'

'Abdul has?'

'And Suleiman. And Salah. And Rafig – Rafig tried to seize her, but she slipped from his grasp and ran out into the yard and jumped over the wall.'

'Jumped over the wall? This tale goes from fancy to wildness. Why, the wall is as high as a man!'

'I know how high it is,' said the omda, nettled. 'And I

75

know she jumped over it. It wasn't just Rafig who saw her. Salah was walking in the road outside when she rose over the wall and came down at his feet. He thought it was a djinn come to take him. But then she laughed and ran off into the sugar cane. And when Salah came to himself he ran to Rafig's door and called to him, and there was Rafig already standing there, bemused.'

'This is nonsense!' said Mahmoud.

'And then,' said the omda, 'they sent a boy for me and when I came we found that things had been taken. As in the other houses.'

'As in the other houses?'

'Not just that night but other nights. Since Ramadan there has been a spate of such robberies. People have taken to barring their doors. But what good is that when she jumps over the wall?'

'This is just some thief,' said Mahmoud, after a pause. 'An ordinary thief.'

'Not that ordinary,' retorted the omda.

'Maybe not,' conceded Mahmoud. 'Nevertheless, there is no need to talk of a Cat Woman.'

'It is not I who talk of a Cat Woman,' said the omda cunningly. 'It is what people say.'

'Well, I say that it is foolishness,' said Mahmoud, 'and I am surprised to hear you, an omda, repeating it.'

'You asked me for a reason why the woman's body was found where it was,' said the omda, 'and I am but giving you an answer: the Cat Woman was taking back her own.'

7

'The provinces,' said Mahmoud darkly, 'are very backward.'

Owen could tell that the Cat Woman rankled. It was an affront to everything that Mahmoud believed in: rationality, progress, the essential equality of Egyptians with people in more developed nations. It was yet another example of Egypt falling short.

'What hope is there for Egypt,' said Mahmoud passionately, 'when people believe such things? Even an intelligent man like the omda? It is ignorance, ignorance that is holding them back.'

'But that can be remedied,' said Owen.

'Yes, I know. Education. Well, yes, I agree we need more of that, and better. But even then! What hurt me most,' he said, 'was that mamur. Because, you see, he *has* had education. Training, certainly. But what use has he made of it? It is not so much his stupid prejudices as his inability to proceed professionally – despite his training! Where are the questions? How could it be suicide? Was someone helping her? Where did the arsenic come from? Did someone have a motive for murdering her? How might the poison have been administered? None of these questions did he ask! His mind was quite closed. It comes as a shock,' Mahmoud confided, 'to find such incompetence. But then,' he went on gloomily, 'it is not just confined to the provinces. As you yourself know.'

Owen, who knew Mahmoud's mood swings well, could tell that he was beginning to work himself into a stew. This was the other side of that enormous drive and passion for perfection – a proneness to fall into depression when things did not work out exactly as he felt they should. To distract him, he said:

'I think I can help you, on one thing at any rate – the identity of the man who sang.'

He told Mahmoud about Fricker.

'When was he down there?'

'I don't know exactly. Some while ago.'

'I don't think he can have had anything directly to do with it,' said Mahmoud. 'However, it would be interesting to talk to him.'

'Would you like to?'

'Could you arrange it?'

'Certainly. I'll get you a permit to visit the camp.'

On second thoughts, perhaps that was not a good idea. There were only Germans in the camp, no Egyptians; even so, Mahmoud might well take exception to the notion of the camp, indeed, to its very existence in what he believed should be an independent, neutral country.

'No, I'll tell you what, I'll have him brought up to Cairo. He'll probably be glad of the outing.'

'Would that be possible? Thank you.'

Owen told him what he had been able to find out about Hilde Langer.

'That, too, is very helpful. Although I believe that the reasons for her death are to be found not in Cairo but in Minya.' He grimaced. 'Unfortunately.'

'You will be going back there?'

'In a day or two, yes. And then I shall have to stay. Until it is sorted out.' He grimaced again. 'Aisha will not be pleased.'

He looked at his watch.

'I must go. She will be expecting me.'

Yes, he had changed, thought Owen.

Zeinab was still not speaking to him. At night she embraced him passionately but angrily and then turned away.

Tonight she couldn't sleep. It was exceptionally hot and after a while he got out of bed, soaked some towels in the bath and then hung them across the open doorway leading

78

on to the balcony. It never worked, but some people swore by it.

He got back into bed.

'I saw Mahmoud today,' he said.

Zeinab stared implacably at the ceiling.

'Aisha is well.'

Zeinab quite liked Aisha now, even though she was only about half her age. There was no response, however.

'Mahmoud is a reformed man. He goes home of a night.'

Zeinab turned away on to her shoulder.

'The case he's working on has musical connections.'

Zeinab was sometimes interested in cases with musical connections.

Not tonight.

He told her anyway.

'A promising musical career . . .'

Not a flicker.

'Of course, it will probably turn out to be a case of domestic violence –'

'I can understand that,' said Zeinab unpromisingly.

' – made more difficult by him being an Egyptian and her being –'

Zeinab put the pillow over her head.

Owen gave up and turned away from her.

'When did you say she was in Cairo?' said Zeinab.

Zeinab knew the Cairo musical scene. Apart from being an ardent opera-goer, she numbered quite a few musicians among her artist friends. Zeinab had many artist friends. This was chiefly because they were the only people disreputable enough to allow women to mix with them on a basis of equality.

'About ten to fifteen years ago. Before your time,' said Owen.

'I will speak to Hussein. Perhaps he will remember her.'

'I don't think she would have been –' how was he going to put this? ' – part of Hussein's musical world.' Hussein, as far as he remembered, was, or considered himself to be, very avant-garde. 'From what I can gather, she played mostly at private musical evenings. Soirées. For the German community.'

'I am beginning to feel quite friendly towards Germans,' said Zeinab, putting the pillow back over her head.

Cavendish was in the bar, talking to McPhee. He turned towards Owen as he came in.

'Hello,' he said, 'we were talking about you. McPhee tells me you're on to something.'

'The ghaffirs? Well, I don't know –'

'It sounds as if it could be something big.'

'Oh, I wouldn't say that –'

Cavendish smiled.

'Not until you're quite sure, is that it? Very wise of you. But anything that touches a Minister is big. And doubly big, just at the moment, if it's the Minister of the Interior.'

'Well, I don't know. I recently talked to the inspector involved and, I must say, I came away feeling that he hadn't got any deep designs.'

'But, Owen,' said McPhee, 'he may have been just an unwitting tool.'

'He wrote the report, didn't he?' said Cavendish. 'Not so unwitting.'

'If Owen thinks he's sound,' said McPhee loyally, 'then he probably is.'

'Well, I wouldn't go so far as –' said Owen. 'And as a matter of fact, I've learned something about him since which has surprised me.'

'You have? And it made you think?' Cavendish nodded his head approvingly.

'He's behind bars, anyway,' said McPhee. 'No, it's the others I'm worried about.'

'Others?' said Cavendish.

'The ones who originally commissioned the report, then immediately accepted it, and who are now busily implementing it!'

'Hmm,' said Cavendish thoughtfully.

'And who appointed six Germans to senior posts within the Ministry,' said McPhee triumphantly.

'That was probably McKitterick,' said Owen.

'McKitterick?' said Cavendish.

'The Adviser.'

'The Adviser! And he appointed them?'

'It doesn't necessarily mean anything,' said Owen hastily. He began to regret that he had spoken.

'It ought to be looked into.'

'I really don't –'

Cavendish took out a notebook and wrote the name down.

'Look,' he said to Owen, 'I know you're busy. McPhee has told me about all this internment stuff. Why don't you let me look into McKitterick for you?'

'Well, thank you, but –'

He couldn't do this!

On second thoughts . . .

'Well, I'm not sure that I –'

'No, really. It would be no trouble at all.'

Why not? McKitterick was an arrogant sod who had it coming to him, and it would keep Cavendish happy. He wouldn't find anything out because there was nothing to find out, so no harm would be done.

'Well, thank you,' he said.

'Not at all. This is important. I'll tell you what: why don't I have a word with my people back in Whitehall and get them to free you? It's ridiculous you being busy with this internment stuff when there's something like this you should be following up.'

'That would be most helpful –'

'We need you down in Minya.'

Minya! Owen wasn't so sure about that.

What, apart from anything else, would Zeinab say?

Plenty.

'You don't love me. All you want to do is get away from me!'

'Nonsense! The idea came from him.'

'I'll bet you put it in his head.'

'I certainly didn't! What the hell do I want to go to Minya for? It's hot and sweaty and sticky –'

'Is there a woman there?'

81

'No, there's not a woman there! Look, I don't want to go. I want to stay here with you.'

'You're practising,' said Zeinab. 'Practising for the time you go away altogether and get killed.'

'No, I'm not! Listen, I don't need to go there for long.'

'I don't care how long you go for. You can go there for ever, as far as I'm concerned.'

'I don't even have to go there at all. It's a crazy idea. There's nothing to it!'

'Then why are you going?'

'I told you. That bloody fool, McPhee –'

'You always blame McPhee.'

'– sold Cavendish this crazy notion that a conspiracy –'

'The British always go on about conspiracies. When they are the worst conspirators of the lot!'

'Yes, well . . .'

'You,' said Zeinab, 'are conspiring against me!'

'How am I conspiring against you?'

'You're plotting,' said Zeinab. 'You're plotting how to get away.'

'Nonsense!'

'Well, go, then!' she shouted. 'Go to your woman down in Minya!'

Owen had no intention of going. Being freed from all this internment business was one thing; going down to Minya on some wild-goose chase was quite another. He didn't believe for one moment that there was a conspiracy of the sort that McPhee thought. Besides, he hadn't been officially freed from the internment work yet. And besides that, there were plenty of more sensible things that he could be doing in his office.

Most of his mail had been delivered by hand and was therefore unstamped, which made the letter from Alexandria stand out. He picked it up and opened it. It was in an old-fashioned, copybook hand and, although it was written in English, some of the letters were not formed in the usual English way.

Dear Captain Owen, it read:

82

I was very sorry to hear of the death of Hilde Langer. I remember her as a pretty little flaxen-haired girl running around the garden, ours as well as the Knippers', who were next door. She always seemed so full of fun that it is hard to imagine all that energy and bubble cut off – at so young an age, too! I must say, I had my misgivings when she decided not to go back with the Knippers but to stay in Egypt. It is very hard to be a woman on your own in this country, as I have found since the death of my husband. But how much easier for me, as a married woman with a house and friends, than it must have been for her!

In answer to your letter: yes, we have kept in touch. Hilde wrote regularly to me at least twice a year, at Christmas and, usually, in the summer just after my grandchildren had gone back from their holidays and she knew I would be feeling low. There was a whole burst of letters last year when she herself was going through an unhappy period, but then they dried up and I haven't heard from her for some time. Indeed, I was rather expecting a letter from her when yours came instead.

You ask me if I can throw any light on her state of mind. I have already told you that about six months ago she was very unhappy. It was a period of strain in their marriage, not because of tensions between Aziz and her – they loved each other dearly – but because of circumstances. I am sure you are aware that when they returned to Egypt, Aziz's mother came to live with them, as is normal in Egypt. Unfortunately the rest of the family decided to come too and I think – well, it was not what Hilde had expected.

They managed all right for a time, but then things came to a head. Oddly, it was over the piano. You see, there it was, virtually taking up an entire room which they thought could be made better use of. They were used to sharing, you see, and couldn't understand why a room should be set aside for the use of one individual.

83

But Aziz insisted. He knew what it meant to her. And besides, I think he felt guilty that things had not worked out better in Uganda and that they had had to settle for this. She had had to give up so much, you know – at least, that is what I think he thought, he was always such a *nice* man – that he couldn't ask her to give up this. And so he put his foot down, which was most unlike him.

I think, actually, that, for the sake of peace and quiet, she would have been prepared to share the room with them, but he was adamant.

In fact, of course, she was rather glad. The piano had become a lifeline for her. It was the only thing that connected her now with that other life that might have been hers. I don't mean just our comfortable European way of living – she didn't care a scrap for that – but the world of music and art and intellectual life which had once been so important to her. (Did you know she had hoped to become a professional musician?) It wasn't so much that she wanted to go back to that life as that she needed to know it was there. Otherwise, she said, life became impossibly narrow.

I think I know what you want to ask me. *Did* life become impossibly narrow for her? Did it become more than she could bear?

I don't know how to answer; except to say that while she and Aziz were together, no, I don't think it was more than she could bear.

I do feel, looking back over my letter, that I have not helped you at all. Your news has come as such a shock to me. Perhaps when I can think more clearly, I will write to you again.

He took the letter home with him, with the vague intention of dropping it off at the Ministry of Justice, so that Mahmoud could see it. In fact, as he was going through the Midan Abdin he saw Zeinab ahead of him, waiting for an arabeah, so they took one together. He told her about the letter and then, as she seemed interested, let her read it.

Zeinab's sympathies were easily aroused. Initially they had been caught by the fact that the German woman had been a musician; now, though, she began to enter imaginatively into what life had been like for Hilde Langer down in Minya. What – with her own wide artistic interest – struck her now was the painful narrowing that Hilde Langer had experienced.

'And all for love,' she said. She looked at Owen pointedly. 'I don't think I would do that for love,' she said.

'Fortunately, you're not being asked to.'

'No. But suppose you got a job as Mamur Zapt in the Aleutian Islands?'

Owen tried to think where the Aleutian Islands were.

'I don't think they have Mamur Zapts up there,' he said.

'And anyway you're going to the war,' said Zeinab. 'Yes, I know.'

Owen wisely held his peace and they drove on for some time in silence.

Then Zeinab said:

'What made it go wrong?'

'Well, the family –'

'No, no,' said Zeinab, shaking her head impatiently. 'Before that. In Uganda, or even before. What made it necessary for them to have to come back and live like that?'

'Money,' said Owen. 'It's usually money.'

'Yes,' said Zeinab thoughtfully, 'that's where marriages often go wrong. Especially if it's between two people from very different backgrounds.'

'It's where one of them has to move to something different from what they're used to. It comes as a surprise, I suppose.'

'Yes.'

'It won't be like that with us,' said Owen confidently.

'No,' said Zeinab. 'I've known from the start that you're never going to have any money.'

To his surprise, McKitterick wanted to see him. Nikos said he had rung three times. He rang again a few minutes later and asked if they could meet at the Sporting Club that lunch-time.

85

'I'll buy the drinks,' he said; so Owen knew there was something wrong.

When Owen arrived, McKitterick was already there, sitting alone at a table. He jumped up.

'What'll it be? You're a whisky man, aren't you?'

The bar was almost empty. Even so, McKitterick led him away to a corner.

'Good of you to come,' he said. He fidgeted for a moment or two. 'The fact is,' he said, 'I'm in a spot of bother.'

'Oh, yes?'

'I know I ought to have come to you before. But after what you said, I didn't like to.'

'What I said?'

'About issuing guns to the ghaffirs. You were against it, weren't you? Mind you, I still think it a good idea in principle. But – '

He stopped and swallowed.

'Something gone wrong?'

'There's been an over-issue,' said McKitterick miserably.

'I'm sorry, I don't . . . ?'

'When we started implementing the new policy, we put in a big order for guns. Really big. It took up a sizeable chunk of our budget. But we thought, if we're going to do this, we'd better do it properly. So we put in a big order. Not for fifty thousand at once – our budget wouldn't run to that. But for ten.'

He looked at Owen.

'We thought we'd do the south first, you see, where there was more need of guns. And then extend it by stages to the rest of the country.'

'How many have you issued so far?'

'All ten thousand. We thought we'd better crack on with it because we could see we were going to be short-staffed, in the key places, at any rate.'

'With the Germans going, you mean?'

'That's right. So we pushed on with it.'

'And?'

'Well, we got them all out, as planned. But then, well, you have to check these things, you know, if only for audit purposes. One of our chaps made a check and found that there were more guns issued than there were ghaffirs.'

'Significantly more?'

'Two hundred.'

'Two hundred!'

'It's not a lot on ten thousand,' said McKitterick defensively.

'Still . . .'

Still it would send the Administration berserk. Allowing guns to leak out unaccountably into the civilian population, given the strength of the Nationalist movement in Egypt, was about the most heinous crime an official could commit.

'I should have told you at once,' said McKitterick miserably.

He certainly should. Since most leaks occurred from military armouries (sold by the soldiers for drink) and the Army was in a somewhat ambiguous position when it came to investigation, successive Consul-Generals had decreed that any disappearance of arms was to be reported at once to the Mamur Zapt, who would personally conduct the investigation.

'But, knowing how you felt . . . And not wanting to waste your time . . . Well, I thought we'd better make another check first.'

'And?'

'We sent down one of our brightest. And he found it was absolutely true. We'd over-issued in Minya province. I couldn't believe it! I don't know how it could have happened. We have a whole system in place to stop this kind of thing occurring. Procedures, checks, double-checks – I still can't believe it!'

'But they've gone?'

'It – it rather looks like it.'

And unless Kitchener had softened remarkably during his holiday in England, so, very shortly, would McKitterick.

'It's my responsibility, I know,' said McKitterick despondently, 'and I shall have to stand the consequences. I shall inform the C-G's office tomorrow. But first I wanted to tell you.'

'You can say you've told me,' he said generously. 'I shan't tell them when you told me unless they ask.'

'Thanks, Owen. Thanks.'

'I doubt if anything will happen until Kitchener gets back,' said Owen encouragingly, 'so we've got a bit of time, and maybe if we sort this thing out –'

'They're on to me already,' said McKitterick, depressed.

'They?' said Owen. He was surely the only 'they' as far as disappearance of arms was concerned. And 'already'?

'Cavendish. That bloke from Constantinople. He's been sniffing around. Making inquiries.'

'Oh!' said Owen, guiltily.

8

The repercussions began to reverberate through the Administration. Cavendish was the first to ring.

'Owen,' he said, 'Trevelyan has just told me. Apparently
he had a note from McKitterick this morning. Two hundred
rifles! What *is* the Ministry up to? Nothing good, I suspect.
But we've had our suspicions, haven't we? You're going
down to Minya, of course.'

'Of course.'

'Half expected to find you already gone.'

'Er, um, yes, well, shortly. Very shortly.' Inspiration came
to him. 'Still waiting to get shot of all this internment stuff.'

'It's not come through? Good Lord, I'll get on to them
right away. But, look, you don't have to wait for that. I'll
see you get authorization. It's just a case of putting someone
else on to it, isn't it? How about that strange Scottish fellow?'

'McPhee?'

'Is that his name? I'll see about getting the duties transferred. You'll want to be off, won't you? It sounds as if
Minya's the place to go, doesn't it? You were on to that very
early. Smart of you. Look, I'm glad I managed to catch you.
There's a thing I want to ask you. You remember that inspector you mentioned?'

'Fricker?'

'That's the one. Any chance of having a word with him?'

'I'm having him brought up to Cairo tomorrow, as it
happens.'

'You are? You don't waste time, I must say. Perhaps we
could see him together? Then I'll know just where you've
got to. I want to be as much help to you as I can on this.

89

Oh, and there's one other thing. In confidence, you know. What about this chap, McKitterick? Shall I take him in? Before he does any more harm . . . ?

'Leave him, you think?' He chuckled. 'So you can keep an eye on him, is that right? You never know where it may lead! Wise man! Well, I'll go along with you. You're the man – about the only one out here, I can tell you! – who seems to know what he's doing!'

Then it was the Sirdar, the Commander-in-Chief.

'Owen, this is serious. Two hundred rifles! The latest model, too. We could do with a few of those ourselves. Do you know what we're currently issuing? Indian Army rejects. And that's to people who could be going out to fight tomorrow!

'But, look, what I really wanted to say is: what the hell are you doing about it? That's a lot of fire power to go missing, Owen. Who could be wanting to make use of it? And who against? Not us, I hope. Jesus, Owen, that's too much fire power to be wandering about behind your back when you're trying to fight a war!'

And then there was the Financial Adviser, Cunningham, whose memo Owen had still not answered. He tried to signal to Nikos that he wasn't in, but Nikos merely smiled and held out the phone to him.

'Two hundred, Owen! This is very serious. It's a big gap in the stock valuation and Whitehall will be jumping down our throats. And it's not long till the end of the financial year, not in accountancy terms, that is – '

Relieved, Owen assured him that while it might not be long in accountancy terms, it was quite a while in policing terms and that he had every hope of the arms being recovered during that period. Then he rang off, quickly.

He went in to see McPhee, to break the news to him.

'But of course, Owen! I'd be very glad to help. I will certainly take over the internment work from you.'

This was decent of McPhee. Owen knew he hated the work as much as he did.

'However,' said McPhee, 'I do feel I ought to warn you: I may not be able to help you for long, I'm afraid.'

'Really?' said Owen, concerned.

Now he came to think of it, McPhee *had* been looking a bit peaky lately.

'The fact is,' said McPhee shyly, 'I have volunteered.'

'Volunteered? For the Army?'

This was ridiculous. McPhee was about a hundred years old. Forty-five at least. They'd never take him.

'Yes.'

'Well, um, jolly good! But – but, you know, the Administration might not be willing to release you. You're needed here.'

'I realize that it would add to your burden. But, you know, I feel that older men ought to go and not – not the younger ones. We've had our lives, or at least a chance to play a bit of an innings, and, well, they haven't.'

'Look, I really –'

'Besides,' said McPhee confidingly, 'at least I can shoot. Whereas a lot of the younger chaps, you know, straight out from England, can't. From what I have seen. Except each other, of course.'

It was clear that Owen was going to have to go to Minya. It was also clear that he would have to tell Zeinab, and he approached their apartment that evening with some misgivings. Things, however, had been moving fast with Zeinab. As, admittedly, they usually did.

She had been to a party that lunch-time to celebrate a sale by one of her artist friends. Sales, sadly, were not so frequent among Zeinab's artist friends as to promote a life of continuous party-going and there were a lot of people there to share his good fortune.

'Alas,' said the lucky artist, 'fortune it is not, and it seemed better to blow it all on one party than to live carefully on it for the next two weeks.'

There were musical friends as well as painting friends present and Zeinab, remembering her promise, inquired of them if they recalled a Hilde Langer.

'Hilde Langer?' said Raoul. 'Yes, I do remember someone of that name. But wasn't that a long time ago?'

'Hilde Langer?' said Hussein. 'That little German girl? Oh, she was no good.'

'Why wasn't she any good?' asked someone.

'Because she wasn't Egyptian?' suggested someone.

'That, too,' said Hussein. 'There are enough foreigners coming in to take Egyptian musicians' work. But, no, it wasn't so much that. It was that she never amounted to anything. It was all pretty-pretty stuff. She used to play at salons, that sort of thing.'

'What's wrong with that?'

'Well, I wouldn't do it.'

'That's because no one would ask you to, Hussein,' said someone mischievously.

'I wouldn't do it even if they did!' retorted Hussein. 'Salon music is the music of privilege.'

'Hilde Langer wasn't privileged,' said Zeinab.

Hussein sniffed.

'Silly, sentimental songs!' he said.

'Schubert? Brahms?' said the mischievous one.

'Yes! The music of foreign privilege!'

'But sentimental, silly?'

'Women's stuff!' said Hussein contemptuously.

'What's wrong with women's stuff?' said Zeinab, taking umbrage.

'It's the music of feeling, Hussein,' said someone. 'That's why you don't like it.'

'It's the music of false feeling!' cried Hussein, getting excited, as he usually did in arguments. 'Lonely, yearning, romantic, young girl's love!'

'Well, she *was* lonely, and a young girl, and in love!' shouted Zeinab, who also tended to fire up in argument. 'What's false about that?'

'Didn't she marry an Egyptian?' asked someone beside her.

'But it's weak feeling, it's a woman's feeling!' roared Hussein. Usually he drank lemonade but this afternoon, in honour of Fahmi's sale, they were all drinking Greek wine. 'It's not feeling as I feel it here!' He beat upon his chest dramatically.

'But it's feeling as I feel it *here*!' cried Zeinab, banging her heart too. She was not in fact at all certain about the music. About the feeling, though, she was absolutely sure.

'She did, but it was the end of her as a musician,' said the person beside her. 'They wouldn't have her after that.'

'Quite right!' shouted Hussein. 'She was *no good*!'

'They shut her out,' cried Zeinab. 'But did you take her in?'

'Certainly not!'

'A fellow musician!'

'She was no good, I tell you!'

'You shut her out,' said Zeinab, who was by this time feeling very protective towards Hilde Langer, 'because she was a woman!'

'And quite rightly, too!'

Zeinab threw her glass at him.

Friends grabbed them both.

'Zeinab, Zeinab!'

'Hussein!'

'She was a young girl on her own,' cried Zeinab, 'and you shut her out! They shut her out and then you shut her out. You bastards!'

And walked unsteadily out of the room.

She was still spitting fire when Owen came tentatively into the apartment.

'The bastards!' she said indignantly.

'What is it now?'

'Hussein and the others. They shut her out. Just because she was a woman!'

Owen took a look at her and then went into the kitchen to fetch her a tumbler of water.

'Who's this?'

'Hilde Langer. That German woman. They wouldn't take her in when the Germans threw her out. Because she was a woman.'

Owen, who knew most of her friends, tried to make peace.

'It may not have been because she was a woman. It could have been for all sorts of reasons. Because she was a foreigner. Or, look, you know what Hussein is. I told you he probably wouldn't like her kind of music.'

Zeinab shook her head.

'It was because she was a woman.'

She finished the water and let her head fall back on the cushion and closed her eyes.

Then she opened them again and tried to sit up.

'I have feeling!' she said fiercely.

'You certainly do.'

He pressed her back against the cushions and put his arm round her.

'They didn't want her because she was a woman!' said Zeinab.

Owen pulled her towards him.

'I want you because you're a woman,' he said.

Zeinab considered this, trying to focus her eyes on a spot on the ceiling. Then she yielded and allowed herself to be pulled.

Owen thought she might go to sleep, but her eyes remained open. She seemed content to lie against him, however, and he thought this might herald an improvement in relations.

Zeinab's eyes focused firmly.

'Of course, you'll be going to Minya,' she said.

Fricker had been brought up to Cairo the day before and lodged in a cell overnight. Owen wasn't sure about this, but then he wasn't sure about any of the provisions for internees. Fricker was hardly a criminal, so why should he be lodged in a cell? Couldn't he be given bail or something? But no, the Aalim Zapt, his Legal Adviser, said, he couldn't be given bail because he wasn't a criminal. So the cell it was.

And then where should he be questioned? The interrogation rooms at the Bab-el-Khalk were bare and hardly friendly. Mahmoud, he was sure, would prefer somewhere more relaxed. Fricker to him was a witness, not an enemy. But then, after Mahmoud, Cavendish would interview him, and to Cavendish Fricker *was* an enemy.

He considered having him brought to his own room,

which would be more congenial. But then Mahmoud refused to recognize the office of Mamur Zapt and would feel his position prejudiced. In the end Owen persuaded McPhee to let him use his office. Mahmoud wouldn't mind this since he did recognize the post of Deputy Commandant of the Cairo Police and was, indeed, prepared to accept the Bab-el-Khalk – as police station, that was, not as residence for the Mamur Zapt.

Mahmoud arrived first. They heard Fricker coming along the corridor and then a guard brought him in. They both rose.

'Mr Fricker, Mr el Zaki,' said Owen. 'Mr el Zaki is from the Parquet and would like to ask you a few questions.'

'The Parquet?' said Fricker, surprised. He shook hands.

'Yes. It concerns the case of a Mrs Hanafi,' said Mahmoud.

'Hanafi? I'm afraid –'

He shook his head.

'Hilde Langer,' said Owen.

'Hilde Langer? But – oh, of course! I had forgotten for the moment. I always think of her as Hilde. Yes, I know her.'

'I am the officer investigating the case,' said Mahmoud. 'I was hoping you might be able to help me.'

'Well, of course. I would be glad to help. But why –?'

'Hilde Langer is dead,' said Owen gently.

Fricker seemed stunned.

'Dead?'

'You did not know?' asked Mahmoud.

'No. I have been away. I –'

He looked at Owen.

'It happened just about the time you were taken into internment,' said Owen.

'Hilde? Dead?'

'I am afraid so, Mr Fricker, I am sorry to press you at a time like this. The news obviously comes as a shock to you.'

'Yes. I saw her – I saw her only a short time ago. She seemed perfectly well. What . . . ? Did you say this was a case? How did she die?'

'We do not know yet.'

'But obviously –?'

95

'We are concerned about the manner of her death. We think, I am afraid, that she was murdered.'

The blood drained from Fricker's face.

'Hilde! Murdered!'

Owen got up and went out of the room to order coffee. When he came back Fricker had buried his face in his hands.

'There is no justice,' he whispered. 'She had had such a hard life.'

He lifted his head.

'It was not Aziz?'

'Why should it be Aziz?'

'No,' said Fricker. 'It wouldn't be. It couldn't be!'

An orderly brought in some coffee.

Fricker took a sip and nodded his thanks. Then he put the cup down.

'Please!' he said. 'If I can help, I would gladly do so.'

'Very well. Let us begin with something you said. That you had seen her a short time ago. When was that?'

'Five, six months ago. I was down in Minya. Looking at the ghaffir system. I am an inspector, you see,' he explained. 'I was writing a report. I stayed there for, oh, two, three weeks. I got to know Aziz. I mentioned to him once that I sing. German songs, I said. "Oh," he said, "then you must meet my wife." Well, I went, not expecting much. But then I found that it was Hilde!'

'You had met her before?'

'Yes, yes. In Cairo. I used to sing, she used to play.'

'At musical evenings for the German community?'

'Yes. At one time, almost every week.'

'You knew her well, then?'

'Yes, of course! We played together, we practised together – much practice. It is necessary to practise together in order to perform together. There must be no gap.'

'No gap?'

'Between the voice and the piano.' He looked wryly at Mahmoud. 'That was all, though. It did not apply to – other things.'

'How long did this go on for?'

'About three months. Then I was posted. I am inspector, you see. Travel much. Travel all the time. When I came back she had gone. "No more Lieder," I think. Well, of course, that was not true. There were other accompanists. But not like her. She – she was perfect.'

'And you never saw her again until this recent visit to Minya?'

'No. I heard she had married. Married an Egyptian. He was in dams, I think. At that time. So when I met him at the sugar factory I made no connection. It was surprise, great surprise to me.'

'Mr Fricker, you said that when you saw Mrs Hanafi again, she seemed quite well?'

'That is so, yes.'

'And happy?'

Fricker hesitated.

'It is difficult,' he said.

'The family?'

'That is so. Very difficult.'

'Aziz?'

Fricker shook his head.

'Between them, no difficulty.'

His English, thought Owen, was not so good today.

'But happy?' Mahmoud pressed him.

'Things were hard for them, very hard.'

'Mr Fricker, when I told you that Mrs Hanafi had been murdered, you said: "It was not Aziz!" As if you thought it could have been Aziz.'

'No! That is not so! That was foolish thought. Foolish thing to say!'

'And yet it was your first thought.'

'That was because there was no one else. No one else that she knew. In that terrible place.'

Owen had wondered how Cavendish would behave towards Fricker, because for Cavendish Fricker definitely was the enemy. There wasn't even the restraint that had operated in the case of Owen when he had talked to Fricker before in the camp, namely that he had been conscious that he was addressing a professional colleague. They were both servants of the Khedive; and they had been able to talk as they had, disagreeing with each other but dispassionate about the subject, because it was something that had arisen in the course of their work and where it was the object of both simply to arrive at a working solution.

In Cavendish's case there was no such restraint. There was this time no shaking of hands. In fact, it was Fricker who set the note. When Cavendish came in he rose to his feet and bowed politely. Cavendish, caught slightly by surprise, and perhaps also because he was accustomed to the diplomatic forms of the Sublime Porte, bowed back. It set a note of polite formality which Owen decided to preserve.

'Mr Cavendish, Mr Fricker. Mr Cavendish has some questions he would like to put to you, Mr Fricker.'

'Of course.' He bowed again.

Cavendish smiled.

'They concern your report, Mr Fricker. Or, rather, the recommendations you made in your report.'

'They were helpful, I hope?'

'Oh, yes. Very helpful.'

'Good,' said Fricker, pleased.

'Mr Fricker, I wonder if you can tell us something about the process within the Ministry which led to the report? Who initiated it in the first place?'

'Well, I think I initiated it,' said Fricker. 'The idea came to me one day when I was down at Beni Sueif. I had been looking at the ghaffirs, and I thought: "This is hopeless! There is no system." And then I thought, well, what sort of system should there be? And then when I got back I prepared a little paper, and, well, things followed from there.'

'They liked your paper?'

'Oh, yes.'

'Who, particularly?'

'Well, Mr McKitterick circulated it to all the important people, I think.'

'The Minister?'

'I believe so.' Fricker smiled, pleased. 'Yes, I believe so.'

'Any names in particular?'

'I think the report received general support,' said Fricker seriously.

'Among the senior people?'

'Yes.'

'But especially Mr McKitterick?'

'He has always been most receptive of my ideas.'

'I see. Thank you. The reason I am asking, Mr Fricker, is that I am very impressed. It is not often that one moves so swiftly from idea to implementation.'

Cavendish was no fool, thought Owen, and he knew more about bureaucracy than Owen had given him credit for. Perhaps that was one of the advantages of working at the Ottoman capital.

'That is so, yes. Very swift. And unusual, too; yes, you are right. The right idea at the right time?'

'I think that may very well be so.'

'I am not always so fortunate with my ideas.' Fricker sighed. 'Usually people say, "Thank you very much," and then nothing is heard of them. The reports of mine that are buried in filing cabinets!'

'Very many, I daresay.'

'And some good ones, I insist.'

'I am sure.'

'There was one especially. When I first started working as inspector. It was on wireless stations.'

'Wireless stations?'

'Yes. A chain of them, all the way down the coast, all the way to East Africa. That is what I suggested. But it never came to anything.'

'An idea before its time, perhaps?'

'Well, yes.' Fricker was pleased. 'That is so. But not long before its time. Nowadays . . .'

But Cavendish cut him short.

'Returning to your proposals about the ghaffirs, Mr Fricker. The trouble with over-speedy implementation is that sometimes things go wrong.'

'That is so, yes,' Fricker agreed.

'As in this case.'

'As in this case?'

'There has been an over-issue of firearms.'

'Well, mistakes occur –'

'By two hundred.'

'Two hundred! No! That is not possible.'

'I am afraid so.'

'But that is not possible. There are controls, safeguards. Signatures. It is not possible!'

'Nevertheless . . .'

Fricker looked worried.

'But this is not possible. Not in terms of the system. The system has been designed – I took very great care –'

'Nevertheless, there has been an over-issue by two hundred guns.'

'But –'

Fricker stopped, now looking *very* worried.

'But this is serious,' he said. 'All those guns!'

'Yes.'

'I cannot understand how it happened. How it *could* have happened. The system –'

'I agree with you,' said Cavendish afterwards.

'About him not having any deep designs?'

'He's just a low-level inspector,' said Cavendish. 'He couldn't have any if he tried!'

9

As the steamer drew into the jetty at Minya, that same jetty from which the Germans whom Owen had rounded up on his previous visit had set out into internment, and where the woman had held out her hands to him, Owen heard shots; not one or two isolated ones but a scattered barrage.

He was the only one who seemed to take any notice. There was a crowd waiting on the jetty: men in long white gowns talking earnestly, women with large bundles on their heads, porters with the skirts of their galabeahs tucked up, waiting to unload and load, and the usual extras in any Egyptian crowd scene, children and beggars. Not one of them turned a head.

There was a policeman standing at the end of the gang-plank. He saluted Owen, the only effendi.

'Those shots,' said Owen, 'what are they?'

The policeman smiled.

'It's the ghaffirs,' he said, 'learning how to shoot.'

A man came pushing up to them.

'Effendi,' he said, 'you want donkey?'

'How far is the mudiriya?'

'Oh, Effendi, too far! Donkey is better.'

'It's the other end of town,' said the constable.

'Only fifty piastres!' said the man.

'Fifty piastres!' said the constable, reeling. There was an audible gasp from the people nearby.

'Fifty it is,' said Owen, in Arabic. 'Milliemes, not piastres.'

'Millienes it is,' said the man, with a broad grin.

They set off up the incline into the town, the man walking beside, leading the donkey, Owen, doubtfully, on its back.

He was used to riding horses but with donkeys the technique was different. You sat well back, perching yourself above its haunches. The ordinary Egyptians sat cross-legged. Owen, unpractised, did not go so far and let his legs dangle down on either side. His feet almost brushed the ground.

The narrow, enclosed street was like an oven. It was full of people, women with great baskets buying vegetables at the stalls, their baskets blocking the way, craftsmen sitting outside their shops sewing leather or turning pegs with a bow held in their toes, men in doorways chatting. The donkey was frequently brought to a stop. Whenever it stopped, a swarm of flies rose from the patches of dung on the ground and settled on the donkey's head, the driver's arms, and on Owen's sleeves. Overhead, the kite hawks wheeled.

The mudiriya, residence of the provincial governor, the mudir, was on the very edge of the town looking out on to the desert. Next to it was the large white block of the police station and a vast parade ground on which men were drilling. They advanced, turned, wheeled and re-turned, not very expertly. None of them were in uniform. Owen guessed they were the ghaffirs on their training course.

Over to one side were extensive firing ranges, which was where the shooting was coming from. Men were lying down firing enthusiastically at targets, again not very expertly – the sand all round the targets and often quite some distance away was being continually puffed up.

The salvoes came to an end. The instructors shouted out orders and each man put his carbine down on the ground in front of him. The instructors went round checking that the safety catches were on. Then the men got up, picked up their guns and moved on to the next range.

Owen stopped for a moment to watch them. It all came back to him, from those days in India when, as a junior subaltern, he had done these very things himself, gone round checking that the safety catches were on.

The men settled down in their new positions and began firing again. The donkey man put his hands over his ears and grimaced.

'Bang-bang!' he said.

Owen's own ears began to ring and they moved on. How many ghaffirs were there here? Thirty? Forty?

The mudiriya was surrounded by a high, whitewashed wall. Behind it was a courtyard and then the building itself, a long, single-storeyed mud-brick house with a narrow roof thatched with sugar cane jutting out from it to make a kind of verandah.

The mudir was sitting on a wickerwork chair in the shade, his bare feet on a small table. He stood up when he saw Owen and then waved in recognition.

'Again?' he said, smiling. 'Didn't you get them all last time?'

'That's not what I've come for,' said Owen.

'No,' agreed the mudir, still smiling. 'I suppose not.'

They sat down at the table and a man brought them native beer.

'It's the guns, isn't it?' said the mudir.

'That's right.'

The mudir gestured towards the ranges.

'Well, as you can hear, they're all properly in use.'

'Not all of them.'

The mudir finished his glass and poured himself some more.

'Well, that,' he said, 'is just what we need to talk about.'

He filled Owen's glass.

'I'm glad you're here,' he said. 'All I've had so far are paper-pushing effendis who push the paper around so fast you don't know where the hell you are. Then suddenly they stop and say: "Right, you bastard, you're in the shit." When all you've tried to do is exactly what they told you to.'

He put the glass down.

'I'll show you. Abdul!'

A man came out of the house.

'Bring me the papers. The ones we've got out. Everything we've got on those damned guns that are supposed to be missing.'

The man disappeared inside and returned with a file.

The mudir took out a paper.

'Here,' he said. 'This is where it all started. They asked me

103

how many ghaffirs there were in the province. I told them.'
He pointed. 'Eight hundred and fifty. There are a lot of villages in Minya. But there's the number, see? And –'

He pulled out another paper.

'– here is the consignment note that came with the guns when they were delivered. How many? Eight hundred and fifty. They sent me what I asked for. Now . . .'

He rummaged in the file again.

'Where the hell is it, Abdul? Oh, here.' He took out another piece of paper. 'This is the list of ghaffirs. See? Every man jack of them. Listed by name. And beside each name is a tick, which tells you they have been issued with one of the new guns. Not only that. Here –'

He laid his finger on the list.

'– is the column where they say they have received it.'

There were a few signatures in the column. For the most part they had made marks.

'I know what you are going to say: how do we know the marks are genuine? That's just the question Fricker Effendi put to me when we were going through it all beforehand. "Well, how the hell do I know?" I said. "The marks have got to be witnessed," he said. "What, each mark?" I said. "God, we'll be here for hours." "It has to be," he said, "and someone has to sign to say they've witnessed." So,' said the mudir triumphantly –

He took up the pages and showed them one by one to Owen.

'At the bottom of each page Abdul has signed it, to say he has witnessed the marks. That's right, isn't it, Abdul?'

Abdul nodded.

'And here, believe it or not, is Osman's signature. Osman is the chief instructor. *Two* signatures. As Fricker Effendi said. He said that was very important. "The system's got to be watertight," he said. "Otherwise someone will land you in the shit." And, do you know, he was dead right. Because that boss-eyed little prick from the Ministry came down and reckoned he'd found two hundred guns were missing. Two hundred guns! "What a load of bollocks!" I said. "We've got a system here, set up by one of your own men, Fricker

Effendi, and I can tell you it's bloody watertight. Eight hundred and fifty I asked for, eight hundred and fifty I received. Eight hundred and fifty I issued. So what's all this about guns that are supposed to have gone missing?"'

Owen went through it all again inside, this time alone with Abdul. He wasn't good with paperwork – Nikos was the man for that – but as far as he could see, everything was in order. So what *was* all this about guns that were supposed to have gone missing?

It was extremely hot in the clerk's office. It was small and airless. There was one tiny window, high up in the wall, looking out on to the courtyard.

Abdul went out to refill the water jug and Owen began to go through the papers once again.

From outside, through the window, he heard the sound of people arriving and then what seemed like the beginning of an altercation.

'You again, you little prick? What the hell are you doing here?'

'I've come to go through your files again.'

'Again? You've done it twice already! Haven't you bastards up in Cairo got anything better to do?'

'Not when two hundred guns have gone missing, no.'

'They haven't gone missing! It's only on paper that they've gone missing. Your paper.'

'That's right,' said another voice. 'Our paper. Something you can rely upon.'

'Oh, you've come, too, have you? What's that for? To hold his hand?'

'To find out how it comes about that your paperwork differs from ours.'

'If there's any difference, it'll be because you bastards up in Cairo have got it wrong! Hello, here's another of them! What the hell do you want? Are you from the Ministry, too?'

'A different Ministry,' said a new voice. 'Finance.'

'A different one! My God, the whole Government will be here soon. Is there something the matter up in Cairo? The plague, or something? Haven't you lot got anything to do?

105

I know what it is! It's got a bit hot, and you've said to your-selves, oh dear, it's all getting a bit too much for me, I think I need a holiday. And then off you go. Brought your families with you, have you?'

'If we were going on holiday, it wouldn't be to Minya, I can tell you.'

'No, I'll bet it wouldn't. Minya is the asshole of the world to a person like you, isn't it? I wish I had your job! Well, let me tell you something: there's someone here already going through the files. The Mamur Zapt. So if you're expecting me to slip you something, if that's the big idea, then you'd better think again. And you can tell that to whoever it was that sent you!'

They filed into Abdul's office a few minutes later, three Egyp-tians, all in the dark suits of the city and all dripping with sweat. The short one in spectacles, Latif, must be the boss-eyed little prick who had first spotted that something was wrong. The taller one, Hoseini, smarter, more politically wise – one of the Ministry's brightest and best, according to McKit-terick – was the one McKitterick had sent down to check. The third one, Kattim, was from the Ministry of Finance and this was his first time in Minya.

'And last, I hope,' he said, mopping his forehead.

'Abdulla has asked us to take him through the books,' said Latif.

'You won't find anything,' warned Hoseini. 'That clerk of his knows his stuff.'

'We'll see,' said Kattim, slightly condescendingly, Owen thought. 'If there's something funny going on, it usually shows up somewhere in the books.'

'*Is* there something funny going on?' asked Owen.

'There's certainly something funny going on with the paperwork,' said Latif. 'There were two requisition notes.'

Requisition notes? He didn't recall seeing one of those in the paperwork the mudir had shown him.

'It's what starts the process,' Hoseini explained. 'In accounting terms, at least. It says how many guns are required.'

'Eight hundred and fifty?' said Owen. He'd got it now.

'Well,' said Hoseini, 'he sent in two of them. The first was for eight hundred and fifty. The second, which was for one thousand and fifty, came in afterwards.'

'They thought it was an amendment,' said Latif, 'so that was the one they worked to.'

'Sending one thousand and fifty?'

'That's right.'

'According to our people,' said Hoseini. 'But not according to the mudir. He denies having sent the second note. He says he only asked for eight hundred and fifty.'

'Which was what he got,' said Owen. 'According to the consignment note.'

'That's a bit of a puzzle, too,' said Latif. 'The ship's captain says he never saw it. He doesn't work to notes, anyway. As far as he's concerned, he just loads and unloads. The checking is done on shore at both ends.'

'A shipping clerk did the checking at the Cairo end,' said Hoseini. 'He worked to our paperwork and the consignment note for one thousand and fifty. He's adamant that one thousand and fifty were loaded.'

'What about at the Minya end?' asked Owen.

'That's where the consignment note for eight hundred and fifty comes in,' said Latif. 'They say that was the one that was with the cargo and they worked to that.'

'Was not the first requisition note cancelled when the second one came in?' asked Kattim.

There was a little silence.

'Apparently not,' conceded Hoseini.

'It ought to have been,' said Kattim severely.

'But that doesn't explain the consignment note,' said Owen.

'I suspect,' said Hoseini, 'that, just as there were two requisition notes, so there were two consignment notes. The shipping clerk in Cairo worked to ours for one thousand and fifty, and a quite different one, for eight hundred and fifty, was produced at the Minya end.'

'The two hundred guns disappearing in between?'

Hoseini shook his head.

'I think it more likely,' he said, 'that they went on to Minya and were unloaded there with the others. Then all that would be necessary would be to switch the consignment notes and send the second one to the mudiriya together with the eight hundred and fifty guns originally asked for.'

'And the others?'

Hoseini smiled.

'That, I think, Mamur Zapt, is a question for you, not for us.'

Owen decided to leave them to it. The office was too small for them all to work together comfortably and, besides, they were clearly much better at this sort of thing than he was. These finance people were all the same: like terriers. Once they got their teeth into something they didn't let go. The thought of that long unanswered memo back in his office came uncomfortably into his mind.

He emerged blinking into the sunlight of the courtyard. The mudir was back in his chair in the shade, a fresh bottle of beer on the table before him. He looked gloomily up as Owen went past.

'You see how it is, Effendi? Three of them! And all here for one reason only: to show that whatever went wrong, went wrong at this end and not up in Cairo. The bastards!'

On the way out he went past the ranges again. The ghaffirs were still firing away. He stopped again to watch them, feeling twinges of nostalgia. It was all so familiar.

Then a thought suddenly struck him. Ought it to be?

He walked over to one of the instructors.

'What ranges are you firing at?'

'Two hundred yards, five hundred, and up to a thousand, Effendi.'

'Aren't those ranges a bit long for ghaffirs?'

The instructor shrugged.

'It's what we were told to practise on, Effendi.'

'Those are military ranges.'

The instructor shrugged again.

*   *   *

The afternoon heat lay over the town. The streets were deserted. Only down by the river were there people, a few women with baskets on their heads, who, having taken their produce to the market, were waiting for the ferry to go home to the other side of the river.

The constable came sauntering down.

'Hello, girls!' he said. 'Have you got anything for me?'

'What would we have for you, Mustapha? Our baskets are empty.'

'I wasn't thinking of what you carry in your baskets.'

'What *could* he be thinking of?' said one woman to another.

'I don't know. Melons, do you think?'

'No, I think it must be bananas. One particular banana, at any rate.'

'Now, now, girls! I just thought you might fancy a happy moment before you went home.'

'I really don't know what you're talking about, Mustapha. I shall have to ask your wife.'

The ferry was just putting out from the other side of the river. It was a heavy, ungainly boat with a squat, square sail, quite unlike the graceful feluccas with their curved lateen rigs. For some time it hardly seemed to move. From somewhere across on that side came the faint bleating of goats.

On this side of the river all was still. There wasn't a movement in the town. The waterfront, which had been so crowded when he arrived, was empty, apart from the women, fallen silent now, and a solitary tea seller higher up the bank, sitting beside his brazier oblivious of the heat, his teacups spread out on the sand in front of him. From somewhere, far away, came the faint drone of an engine.

Owen could see the ferry more clearly now. The goats seemed to be on it. He could see the black-and-white backs milling around.

He watched as it came in. Just before it reached the jetty, the boatman stooped and threw one of the goats over the side. It floundered and splashed for a moment and then made its way to the shore. Then the man threw the others. He ran back to the tiller and turned it into the wind. It lost way and came gently into the jetty. The boatman threw a rope out. The constable caught it and made it fast.

'Hello, Salah,' he said. 'Cheated the crocodiles again, have you?' He peered down into the boat. 'But not for long, I fancy. There seems more water in here than usual. And more shit.'

'There is no more water in here than usual!' retorted the boatman indignantly. 'It just washes in and washes out.'

'Bloody great hole, is there?' said the constable. He turned to the women as they came forward. 'You want to watch out, girls!'

'Thank you, Mustapha. We'll bear your words in mind.'

'Don't worry, Mustapha. As soon as the boat gets going, Salah sticks his behind in the hole and stays there till we get to the other side.'

'Oh, that's all right, then.'

A truck came bouncing along the bank and drove down to the end of the jetty. It must be one of the sugar factory ones, thought Owen. Some workmen jumped out and came down to the ferry carrying their baskets of tools. The driver went across to the tea seller and squatted down.

The workmen greeted the constable and got into the ferry with the women. Two of them held the edge of the jetty while the constable cast off.

He stood for a moment watching the boat put out and then began to make his way up the bank in the direction of the tea seller.

Owen fell in beside him.

'Hello, Effendi. Did you find the mudiriya all right?'

'Yes, thank you.'

The tea seller looked up as they approached.

'Hello, Mustapha.'

The constable seemed to be on good terms with everybody on the waterfront, thought Owen.

'Made your fortune yet, then, Ibrahim?' he inquired.

'It grows greater day by day.'

'Let me add to it, then,' said Owen, laying out some coins on the sand. 'For my friends, too.'

The constable and the truck driver inclined their thanks.

The tea seller put out two little tin cups and poured them both tea from a tall jug with a long spout, then refilled the driver's cup.

'He's been to see the mudir,' the constable informed them.

'Lucky him!' said the truck driver.

The tea seller looked Owen up and down in exaggerated fashion.

'He's still got his trousers on!' he said.

'That's because he's an effendi,' said the driver.

'That old bastard would have the very clothes off your back,' said the constable, grinning.

'He's like that, is he?'

'All mudirs are,' said the driver.

The tea seller looked at him curiously.

'He doesn't bother you, though, Sidi, does he?'

'No,' said the driver, 'he doesn't bother me.' He put his cup down on the sand and made to get up. 'I've got some things to collect for the factory,' he said.

'They're over there at the end of the jetty,' the constable said.

'They can wait,' said the tea seller, refilling the driver's cup.

'They can wait,' agreed the driver, subsiding.

Owen sipped his tea. It was black and hot.

'You were right about the shooting,' he said to the constable. 'When I got there, there were ghaffirs all over the place.'

'There are ghaffirs all over the place all the time these days,' said the tea seller. 'They're always here.'

'It's that training they've got to do,' said the constable.

'Training?' said Owen. 'What does a ghaffir want training for?'

'I don't know,' said the tea seller. 'He never used to.'

'It's these new guns,' said the constable.

'Yes,' said Owen, 'I saw them. Why does a ghaffir need a gun like that?'

'He doesn't,' said the constable. 'It's just one of these daft ideas they have up in Cairo.'

'You know what, though?' said the tea seller. 'They really

111

think they're somebody now. Ever since they got the guns they've been walking around as if the sun shone out of their backsides.'

'They're getting to be a real pain,' agreed the constable.

'What's a ghaffir, after all? We always used to pick the village idiot.'

'Well, that made sense, didn't it? That way you knew they were never likely to make any trouble.'

'It's different now, though. You tell them to bugger off and they don't. I don't know what the world's coming to.'

'They're getting above themselves, and that's a fact,' agreed the constable. He turned to the driver. 'You have any trouble with ghaffirs out your way, Sidi?'

The driver finished his cup.

'No,' he said. 'We don't have any trouble with ghaffirs.'

'You wouldn't, though, would you?' said the tea seller. 'Not out your way.'

10

There were no hotels in Minya and Owen was staying at the Government rest house. It was where officials usually stayed in their tours of the province and he saw Fricker's name higher up the page when he signed the Visitors Book.

The rest house was small – there were only half a dozen bedrooms – but the food was good and it was possible to have guests for meals. Fricker had signed in several. Among them, on no fewer than four separate occasions, was the name Hanafi.

Well, perhaps that was not surprising. He knew that they had met and they had obviously struck up an acquaintance good enough for Hanafi to have invited Fricker to meet his wife. All the same, Owen was a little surprised. Four separate occasions? Over a period of – he looked – less than three weeks. It didn't square with the picture he had had in his mind of the Hanafis living an isolated, closed-in life in that awful house among the sugar cane. Perhaps it was just the wife who had led the isolated life!

Hanafi had, though, taken Fricker over to see her. They had sung together. Just once, or several times? He had the impression that it was more than once.

How had they managed that? The sugar factory was quite some distance from Minya, two hours at least if you went by boat, which would be the normal way. Hanafi would, of course, probably have access to the factory's trucks. Even so, that was a lot of to-ing and fro-ing. These were working trucks.

He looked again at the signings-in. They were all for lunch. That would certainly have helped. There might be a truck coming in regularly to the town, that truck, perhaps, that he had seen down on the waterfront. Hanafi could have come in by that; and then, probably, in the evenings the trucks would not be being used. Fricker would have been fetched and returned.

But then there was another problem. Journeys and lunch would take up the best part of a working day. Four full days in just over two weeks? When Hanafi was a working manager? How had he managed that? Owen hadn't the impression that his boss, Schneider, would look very kindly on that sort of thing!

Unless, of course, Hanafi was coming to Minya on business. But what business was it that would bring him to Minya four times in such a short period?

And had it anything to do with Fricker?

The three Egyptians were also staying in the rest house. They came in when he was halfway through his meal and joined him later on the verandah for coffee. He asked them about their day.

'Fruitless!' said Kattim, mopping his neck with a silk hand-kerchief. He seemed to be troubled by the heat. 'Entirely fruitless!'

'At least you got a feel for the books,' said Hoseini soothingly.

'These provincial bookkeepers!' said Latif, shaking his head with a smile.

'The books are all right,' said Kattim. 'They are consistent with the other documentation.'

'But can that documentation be trusted?' said Latif.

'Can anything here be trusted?' asked Hoseini. 'Including, and perhaps especially, that clerk of his.'

'It's not just the books,' said Latif. 'Don't forget, he was the one who checked the guns in, too. Against the consignment note, he says. But which consignment note?'

'If the consignment notes were switched,' said Hoseini, 'he was the man best placed to do it.'

He looked to Kattim for agreement but the man from the Finance Ministry said nothing. Owen was trying to read the by-play between them. He sensed there was some kind of tension. Was it just the usual tension between Finance and everybody else? Or was there more to it?

Down below them the moon was silvering the river. The palm trees along the bank were black; but then suddenly a puff of wind seemed to catch them and it was as if they were shaking silver sparkles down into the water.

'It's really not so bad here!' said Latif contentedly.

Kattim sniffed.

'Not if you like heat and flies,' he said.

There was a little silence, and then conversation resumed. They talked on for a while and then Latif stood up and announced his intention of going for a walk. Hoseini went with him. Kattim remained sitting.

Owen waited.

'I hate the provinces,' said Kattim. He looked around with disgust. 'I hate the flies, yes, and the dirt and the mosquitoes. But I also hate the ignorance and the stupidity and the narrowness, the general –' he shuddered – 'absence of anything that makes life intellectually interesting.'

He looked at Owen.

'And I know what I'm talking about,' he said. 'Because I grew up in a place like this. When I went to Cairo, to the university, I said, "Never again!" And, fortunately, for the most part, that is how it has been. I hate the provinces. And yet it is not right. It is not right to blame the local officials whenever anything goes wrong.'

'You think the mudir is being unfairly treated?'

Kattim shook his head.

'No,' he said. 'I do not say that. There is clearly something wrong. But I think if I were Mamur Zapt I would be asking myself why is it that the Ministry is so very anxious to show that whatever went wrong, went wrong at Minya. When it seems to me that there are important questions which could be asked at the Cairo end.'

'Such as?'

'Well,' said Kattim, 'why wasn't the original requisition note, the one for eight hundred and fifty guns, cancelled? Why was it allowed to remain in the files, where it could lead to misinterpretation? And then the second consignment note, the one that the mudir's clerk says was with the guns and which he worked to, and which my colleagues at the Ministry of the Interior say is clearly false: have you looked at it?'

'Er, well . . .'

'I have. Carefully. And I was also able to look, back in Cairo, at the dispatch clerk's copy of the other consignment note, the one for one thousand and fifty guns. The second consignment note is also on Ministry paper and is drawn up in exactly the same way. That is to say, by someone familiar with the Ministry's way of doing things. Each Ministry, you know, has its own peculiarities. It has, too, the same internal stamping as the other. You know, "Accounts", "Despatch", etc – each section stamps it as it passes through the system. The stamping appears to me genuine, and I see no reason to suppose that the second note didn't go through the system in exactly the same way as the first.'

'You mean that *both* notes were produced inside the Ministry?'

Kattim smiled.

'I mean only,' he said, 'that if I were Mamur Zapt, that is a question that I would be asking.'

He stood up.

'I think I shall return to Cairo tomorrow,' he said. 'I really do hate the provinces.'

Owen decided to go for a walk himself. Although it was still early in the evening the town was silent. Not like Cairo, thought Owen, when things only began to hum towards midnight. Down by the river, though, there were sounds of merriment, and when he came to the top of the road leading down to the jetty he could see them: about a dozen men, sitting on the end of the jetty, passing a jug between them.

One of them looked up and saw him.

'Hello, Effendi!' he said, with a drunken giggle.

'Hush, Mohammed! Do not be discourteous. He means nothing by it, Effendi. It is just that we are celebrating.'

Owen went down to them.

'What is it that you are celebrating?'

'The end of our course.'

'Ah!' He had worked it out now. 'You must be ghaffirs.'

'That's right, Effendi. We've come in here to learn to shoot.'

'That is, perhaps a good thing, since you are ghaffirs.'

'Oh, I don't know, Effendi. There's not much call for shooting out where I come from.'

'That's not the point, Hussein,' said a new, authoritative – or if not authoritative, at least relatively sober – voice. 'We have to learn so that in case of need we might be called upon. That is what the mudir said.'

'But what need could there be?' asked Owen.

'I don't know, Effendi. To fight against the brigands, I think the mudir said.'

'Ali,' said a voice uneasily. 'I don't think I want to fight brigands.'

'Well, of course, it might not actually come to that.'

'I don't want to fight anybody.'

'Suppose someone attacked the village?'

'I would run and tell the omda.'

'Well, what the hell do you expect him to do about it?'

'I don't know, Ali. But he would tell me what to do.'

'He might tell you to go back and fight them.'

'On my own? Look, Ali . . .'

'Not on your own, blockhead! That's the whole point of getting us together and giving us these guns. If the village is attacked, the omda sends someone to fetch Mohammed from Fazkat and Isa from Arba'im, and the ghaffirs from the other villages nearby, and they all come running –'

'But, Ali, suppose they don't come running very fast?'

'Well, then, you'll just have to fight them off for a while by yourself, won't you?'

'Ali, I think I'd do much better to run off into the sugar cane –'

Owen was up early, as was his custom, and was walking through the town while the smell of new bread was still fresh in the air. He half expected, when he got to the police station, to find no one there yet, but a sleepy constable was sitting on the doorstep drinking tea and in an inner room he found the local chief of police, the mamur he had met at the cat cemetery.

'That was the start of it all,' said the mamur gloomily. 'Oh, Effendi, if only you had come a couple of days earlier. Then none of this would have happened. You would have taken that silly bitch off into prison and we wouldn't have had any of this trouble.'

'Trouble? What trouble?'

'Effendi, I am not one to complain, but there's this little bastard come down from the Parquet, who's making us run around like a donkey with a hot brick up its backside. "What's all the excitement for?" I said to him. "It's only a woman, isn't it?" Well, he gives me a nasty look. "She's been murdered, hasn't she?" "Not only that," I say, "she's a foreign woman." "Foreigners are our guests," he says. "Oh," I say, "that's it, is it? Well, if they're our guests, tell me who invited them? And, anyway," I say, "you can tell what sort of a guest she is, for they send the bloody Mamur Zapt –" sorry, Effendi! – "down from Cairo to take her off to prison!"

'Well, he gets very nasty and says what the hell do I know about it? "Nothing," I say. "I don't come from Cairo." He looks at me in that cold way of his. "The crime occurred in your district, didn't it?" he says. "Yes," I say, "and I'm investigating it." "Oh, good," he says. "Tell me what you've found out, then."

'Now that was a bit of a problem because I've had a lot of other things to do, as I tell him.

' "Did they include the things I asked you to do when I was last here?" he asks, all cold-like.

' "Exactly . . . ?"

' "I asked you to find out where the poison came from," he says.

' "Well, we all know that, don't we?" I say to him. "Old Mother Tayi. She's the one you go to when you want to poison a buffalo. In this village, at any rate. Everyone knows that."

118

'"Did she know it?" he asks.
'"She's in the bloody village, isn't she?" I say.
'"But she was a foreigner. She might not know."
'"Someone in that house would," I say.
'"All right," he says, "then find out who it was."
'"I can hardly ask them," I say.
'"No," he says, "but you can ask Old Mother Tayi."'
The mamur stopped and sighed.

'Well,' said Owen, 'what's wrong with that?'

'It's a lot easier said than done. As you'd know if you met Old Mother Tayi. "Be off with you!" she shouts, and that's before I even get a word out of my mouth. "Be off with you, or I'll put the eye on you!" And she would, too, the old bitch. You don't meddle with Mother Tayi, I can tell you. But how can you expect some stuffed-up little prick from Cairo to know that?'

Owen said that he could see there were difficulties.

'Well, I told him that. And he says, you're bloody useless, get off back to Minya. Not quite like that. These Parquet people are all cold, they never say things straight out. But I could tell that's what he meant.

'"Would you like me to do anything for you in Minya?" I say to him. "Effendi?" Getting at him you see. "Yes," he says, "go to the equivalent in Minya of Old Mother Tayi and find out if the poison was purchased there. If not by the foreign woman, then by anyone else in the family. Including the husband. Especially the husband," he says. "Got that? And I asked you to do that before, too," he says, all cold. The bastard!'

'And have you found out?'

'Yes. No one's bought poison. At least, no one from over that way.'

'Hanafi's been in the town a lot.'

'Yes, and he did go there. But not to buy poison.'

'What did he buy?'

'Something for a headache,' said the mamur evasively.

'Opium?'

'Perhaps. Look, there's nothing wrong with that. Not if you've got a headache. It's not poison. And it wasn't arsenic.'

'Nevertheless,' said Owen, 'if I were you I would tell the man from the Parquet.'

'You think so?'

'I think it might help you with him.'

'Get him off my back?' cried the mamur delightedly.

'And in return,' said Owen, 'perhaps you can tell me something.'

'What do you want to know, Effendi?'

'Hanafi comes into town a lot. At least, he did so when Fricker Effendi was here. You remember Fricker Effendi?'

'The one who sang to Hanafi's wife. Or so he said.'

'The same. Now, you are a man who knows all that goes on in Minya. What did Hanafi come in for?'

'Alas, I do not know, Effendi. I know of his coming in. We used to say that he and the mudir were like blood brothers. At least, that's what I used to say. The others said they must be brothers of the bum, he was in here so often.'

'The mudir? What has he got to do with it?'

'He was the man whom Hanafi always came to see, Effendi. The truck would bring him in and drop him at the mudiriya. I know that because the driver would always come on over here to bring eggs for Agha's wife. That is Agha there, that idle fellow sitting on the doorstep. His wife is the driver's wife's cousin.'

'Do you know what they talked about? Was it business?'

'Alas, I do not know, Effendi. I know only that at that time he was coming in to see the mudir all the time.'

Outside in the courtyard he could hear people assembling.

'It is the ghaffirs,' said the mamur. 'They have come to collect their guns.'

'The guns are kept here?'

'When they are on a course, yes. Otherwise they take them home with them.'

Owen asked if he could see the armoury. A harassed-looking instructor, the one he had talked to on the range, was handing out rifles to a line of ghaffirs. Before handing them over, he checked each one.

'Do you call this clean?' he was saying severely.

'Ibrahim, when I handed it in it was as bright as the morning sun.'

'And now it is as dark as a moonless night. How do you explain that?'

'The air in the armoury, perhaps?'

'The air in your head, Mohammed. Sit there and clean it now.' He looked at Owen. 'They have no understanding, Effendi. Not of guns, at any rate.'

'Guns are a serious matter.'

'That is so, Effendi. And that is what Bimbashi Wickham used to say.'

'You were in the Army?'

'I was, Effendi. And at the end I was in charge of the armoury. "It is a position of trust," Bimbashi Wickham used to say. "And, Ibrahim, you I can trust." '

'He knew his man,' said Owen.

The instructor looked pleased.

'Effendi, I would like to think so. But, please, Effendi, do not judge me by these . . .' Words failed him. 'Effendi, it is not the way that I would have it done.'

'They are not the best of materials.'

'They are good men for their job, but their job is not firing guns. Or looking after them. Effendi, it is not sense to entrust good guns to such as these.'

'You speak the words I would have spoken. Have spoken, indeed.'

'I do my best. I tell them how to keep the guns, I show them how they should be used. And when they come here on courses and bring the guns in, I check the guns and scold them if they have not kept them properly. But, Effendi, I have to scold often.'

'It is not your fault but that of those who have commanded this.'

'Those daft bastards in Cairo,' said the mamur.

'It is not for me to rail against the great,' said the instructor, 'but I really do not see –'

'The mudir said that it was so that they might be used against the brigands,' said Owen.

'The mudir said that?'

'According to the ghaffirs.'

'Against the brigands?' said the instructor. 'The mudir?' He shook his head. 'No, I don't think so.'

'Nor do I,' said the mamur.

'Then for what purpose are they being armed?'

The instructor shrugged.

'Those are soldiers' ranges they're practising at.'

'Yes, but . . . Soldiers? That lot?'

As Owen was walking back through the town he saw the constable he had talked to on the waterfront. He gave Owen a smart salute.

'Hello, Effendi! Are you going down to the river? Then I shall walk with you.'

'It would be a pleasure; but let me not take you from your duties.'

'You do not take me from my duties. They are there as well as here.'

'In fact, if anything happens, I suppose it is more likely to happen there?'

'Nothing happens in Minya,' said the constable.

Owen laughed.

'It is a good place to be, then.'

They came out from between the houses and saw the river ahead of them. There was a large crowd around the jetty.

'The steamer is due,' said the constable.

Owen watched it come in. It was a paddle steamer with two great wheels which splashed water over the onlookers on the edge of the jetty, to the great delight of the crowd. A gangway was run out from the deck and passengers began to file off. Near the rear of the vessel a cover was being lifted off and then a plank was extended and the porters he had seen on his arrival, in their blue beaded skullcaps and with the skirts of their galabeahs tucked up under them, came on board. They went down into the hold and emerged with huge sacks and even packing cases on their shoulders. Then they ran down the plank and deposited them in a flat space at the end of the jetty.

Even before they had finished unloading, men were arriving with donkeys to carry the goods off.

'Is there no man to see that no one goes off with another's goods?' Owen asked the constable.

The constable seemed surprised. He pointed to the crowd jostling around the packing cases.

'There is everyone to see,' he said.

'But suppose the goods have to be counted, or signed for?' said Owen. 'As it was, say, for the guns for the mudiriya?'

'I sent for Abdul and he counted them.'

'Did the steamer wait?'

'It was a special load, so it had to. But the captain said: "Tell Abdul to come speedily, for I cannot wait all day."'

'Even so . . .'

'I think Abdul gave him something, so that he did not mind waiting. Anyway, Abdul wasn't long. He came quickly on his donkey.'

'One donkey? But, then, how did he carry the goods?'

'Oh, he didn't carry them himself, he sent for Abu.'

'Abu?'

'Abu has many donkeys. That is Abu.'

He pointed to a small, wiry man loading sacks on to a pair of donkeys. He saw he was being looked at and waved.

'I would speak with him.'

The constable took him across.

'Abu, the Effendi would speak with you.'

'Let him speak, then.'

'Abu, our friend here says you have many donkeys?'

'I have donkeys enough.'

'Enough to carry many loads?'

'It depends how many. But many, yes.'

'Enough even, say, to carry the guns that came for the mudiriya?'

'He made two journeys,' said the constable.

'Ah, two journeys?'

'The guns were heavy,' said Abu defensively.

'Quite so. Now, Abu, tell me: you made two journeys. Were both to the mudiriya?'

'They were to the police station. That is where they keep the guns.'

'And both journeys were to the police station?'

'Yes, Effendi,' said Abu, puzzled. 'Where else should they be to?'

'No matter. It was just that I wondered. Guns, you see, are important.'

'I know, Effendi. That is what Ibrahim said. ''Guns are a serious business, Abu,'' he said. ''Let no load go astray.'' Ibrahim is the chief instructor up there. And, besides, he knows his business.'

'He does. I have met him. But, now, look, Abu: you made two journeys. What happened to the guns which were left behind while you made the first journey?'

'Nothing happened to them. They were there when I came back.'

'But who watched over them while you were gone?'

'I watched over them,' said the constable. 'And, besides, Abdul was there with his pieces of paper, waving them about and saying: ''Oh, shit!'' '

'Why did he say that?'

'Because he thought one case was missing. It wasn't, but for a few minutes he was really shitting himself, Effendi.'

'And then you came back, Abu, and picked up the guns that remained, and took them to the mudiriya?'

'That is so. And Abdul came with me. Fussing like a hen over its chicks. However, I didn't mind that. For guns are a serious matter.'

The mudir was sitting in his usual place.

'Hello, Effendi,' he said, looking up at Owen and inviting him to sit down. 'One of them's off.'

'Off?'

'Back to Cairo. One of those three bastards.'

'Ah, yes.'

'Had enough of Minya, I suppose. Finds it a bit hot. ''You should be out in the sugar cane,'' I said. ''Then you'd know what heat was!'' ''No, thanks,'' he says, in his lordly way. ''This'll do for me.'' Anyway, he's off. Pity about the other two.'

He produced a bottle of beer from under the chair, where it had been standing in a bucket of water, and gave it to

Owen. 'Drink up, Effendi! You need a lot of liquid down here. The heat sweats all the water out of you.'

Owen took a drink, then put the bottle down.

'The ghaffirs are off today, too, aren't they?'

'Yes. And a damned good thing, too. All this shooting makes your head split. And what's the point? Those useless sods couldn't hit a mountain!'

'They said it was so that they could fight the brigands.'

'Brigands? Bollocks! There aren't any brigands within a hundred miles of here.'

'No?'

'Not to speak of. It was just one of those daft notions that that bloke – what was his name? The one who used to sing to the ladies – Fricker? – had. But you've got to do what he says, otherwise he'll be down here again saying why the hell haven't you done what you were told to?'

'I don't think he'll be down again.'

'No? I wish I could believe that.'

'He's been interned. He's German.'

'You've put him in prison?' said the mudir delightedly. 'Effendi, you've certainly got a head on you! That's the way to treat these Cairo bastards! Drink up, Effendi, drink up –'

11

The truck bounced and jolted its way along the track, throwing up a cloud of dust which came back and made Owen choke. The driver had pulled one of the folds of his headdress over his mouth.

Away to their left was the river, marked by a line of palm trees, but between it and the track was a thin, continuous strip of cultivation which forced them inland to the stonier, sandier ground of the desert. Fellahin were working in the fields and here and there he caught sight of a water-wheel driven by an ox with a small boy on its back.

Here inland there was no cultivation and hardly any people; only, occasionally, they passed someone on a donkey, who would draw aside and look up at them, oblivious to the dust which would immediately surround him.

After about two hours the driver pointed ahead.

'The sugar cane,' he said.

At first Owen could hardly see it, but then he began to make out a long green line which ran across the horizon in front of them. As they approached, it became more definite and now they began to see the tops of dovecotes marking the site of small villages. They never saw the villages themselves, which were too low to show above the fifteen foot high sea of cane.

The track turned along the edge of the plantations and now from time to time they saw houses, small clusters of huts scattered among the sugar cane, sometimes with palm trees around a well or with little irrigation ditches bringing water.

As they came to one of these, Owen saw a small girl

standing in a vegetable patch at the edge of the sugar cane sucking her thumb. She was carrying a gun.

Gun?

'Stop!' he said to the driver.

The truck came to a halt.

'What's she doing?' he said, pointing to the girl.

'Scaring away the crows,' said the driver indifferently.

'Yes, but – that gun!'

'That's to scare them with.'

'Yes, but that's one of the new guns – the ones issued to the ghaffirs.'

'She is a ghaffir,' said the driver.

Owen got out of the truck and went over to the girl.

'Hello!' he said.

'Hello!' she said, removing her thumb from her mouth.

'That's a fine gun,' said Owen.

'It's heavy,' said the girl.

'What are you going to do with it?'

'I know how to shoot it,' said the girl.

'Yes, but who, or what, are you going to shoot?'

'I haven't shot anyone yet,' confessed the girl.

'They've made you the ghaffir?'

'That's right,' said the girl, putting her thumb back into her mouth.

'Where is the omda?' demanded Owen. He had cadged a lift but the truck would have to wait.

The girl pointed to one of the houses, outside which a small group of men were sitting in the shade. Owen strode across.

'Which of you is the omda?'

One of the men signified that he was the headman of the village.

'What are you doing letting them appoint a girl as ghaffir?' said Owen angrily. 'You, a responsible man! This is a disgrace!'

'What's wrong?' said the omda, surprised. 'She's all right. Isn't she?' he appealed to the others.

'She's fine.'

'She's just a girl,' said Owen.

127

'Well, she doesn't have a lot to do.'

'Suppose someone bad came?'

'No one bad comes to this village.'

'In fact, no one comes here at all,' said one of the other men.

It was as Owen had supposed. All a ghaffir was called on to do in the ordinary run of things was to scare away the birds. And to issue them with guns like this! And to call them in for training!

That was another thing.

'What happens when she gets called on to go into Minya for this new training?'

'Training?' said the omda blankly.

'Does not the mudir call her in?'

'We don't have much to do with the mudir,' said one of the men.

'How did she get a gun like this, then?'

'They gave it her,' said the omda.

'Nothing to do with us,' said another of the men.

What about all that stuff at the mudiriya? Fricker's 'careful procedures'? The individual signing out, the witnessing by Abdul and the instructor?

'The gun came with the girl,' said another of the men.

Came with the girl?

'Just a minute,' said Owen. 'Did you not choose this girl yourself?'

'No,' said the omda.

'She's not from the village?'

'No, no. She comes from over Hammadi way.'

Owen had never met anything like this. Usually a ghaffir was chosen from among the members of the village. And although they might, and too often did, choose the village simpleton, they were not usually so cavalier as to pick a stray girl from somewhere else.

'This is a disgrace!' he said sternly. 'I will have to speak to the mudir. Meanwhile, you had better choose another for your ghaffir.'

The omda, and all the other men, looked alarmed.

'Now, hold on –'

'Wait a minute –'

'It's not as easy as that.'

'Of course it is! What the hell's the matter with you?'

'Effendi, it is not quite so straightforward. One does not exactly choose –'

'Not down here –'

'Then what –?'

The omda hesitated.

'One gets . . .' He looked around desperately for inspiration.

'Given?' suggested one of the other men.

'Given,' said the omda gratefully.

'Who by?'

There was a long silence.

'God?' suggested one of the villagers.

'That's it,' said the omda, relieved.

'If God gives, He usually does it through someone.'

They looked at him blankly.

'The factory?'

Was this some kind of company town?

'Factory?' said the omda, puzzled.

'Listen,' said Owen, 'it's got to be somebody. Who put that girl in as ghaffir?'

He couldn't get it out of them. They just sat there woodenly.

'Very well,' he said at last, exasperated. 'On your own heads be it. I shall find out and then there will be trouble. It is monstrous putting a little girl like that up as your ghaffir. Suppose there was big trouble? Suppose the brigands came?'

'Oh, no, Effendi,' said the omda confidently, 'they won't come. Not now that the girl is here.'

The truck turned into the compound and drew to a halt. Owen and the driver got out. It was nearly noon and the workmen were beginning to stop for lunch. He could see them sitting in the shade of the edge of the sugar cane, the big coloured handkerchiefs in which they had brought their bread spread out beside them.

One truck was still being unloaded. Schneider was standing

by the conveyor belt watching the cane being fed in. He turned when he saw Owen and came across, hand outstretched.

'Hell,' he said, 'you here again? What is it this time? Not us, I hope. We're Swiss.'

'I remember,' said Owen.

Schneider glanced at his watch.

'It's lunch-time,' he said. 'Care to join us?'

'Thanks, but I've got a lot to do before I go back. I gather there's a truck going in this evening?'

'About seven. Just a drink, then?'

He took Owen to his office but then, instead of staying there, he picked up a bottle and glasses and took them outside to a small table and two wickerwork chairs standing in the shade of the factory wall. This far south you didn't stay indoors much if you could help it, thought Owen.

'What is it you've got to do?' asked Schneider, pouring Owen a drink.

'I'd like to have a word with Hanafi. Would that be possible, do you think?'

'Oh, yes. He's up and about now. Pulling himself together. He's been in to the factory once or twice. I'm letting him suit himself. No need to be hard on a bloke when he's gone through what Hanafi has. What did you want to see him about?'

'It's something that has cropped up in connection with a job I'm working on in Minya. I'm staying at the rest house and I noticed that at one point Hanafi was there quite a lot.'

'Oh, yes?'

'It was when Fricker was staying there. You remember Fricker?'

'The one who used to sing?'

'That's right.'

'Well, they got quite pally.'

'I wouldn't have looked at it, only he was there during the day. The working day. Four days, in fact. In not much more than two weeks.'

'Not much more than two weeks?'

'I wondered if he was over there on business?'

130

'Four times?'

Schneider looked slightly upset.

'Yes.'

'We do sometimes have business in Minya. But four times!'

'That's what struck me. I wondered if you knew about it?'

'Look, I don't know everything he does, and I don't really want to know, either. I don't like sitting on a man's tail. I like to let him get on with it. But four times in just over two weeks!'

'He also went to see the mudir.'

'I do sometimes send him in to see the mudir. But –'

'What do you send him in to see the mudir about?'

Schneider did not reply at once. He seemed to be thinking.

'Look,' he said, 'my job is to run a sugar factory. And I like to keep on the right side of people. It helps, especially around here. That way you're less likely to run into trouble. Well, from time to time I send Hanafi in to have a chat with the mudir, tell him what we're doing, you know, so that it doesn't come as a surprise to him. If, say, we're going to have an unusual number of shipments going out from the port, and it's going to be blocking up the waterfront for a few days, well, I like to see he knows about it.'

'And that's what it might have been this time?'

Schneider hesitated.

'I don't see how it could have been,' he said reluctantly. 'Not four times in just over a week. If I send him in, it's about once a month.'

'Maybe it wasn't your business but Fricker's?'

'Fricker's?'

'Could it have been anything to do with ghaffirs, do you think?'

'Ghaffirs? Why the hell would he have wanted to talk to Fricker about ghaffirs?'

'Fricker was interested in ghaffirs.'

'Yes, but –'

'The mudir might have been too.'

'Well, maybe, but our business is sugar cane, not ghaffirs.'

131

'So what business was he seeing Fricker on, then? Four times in nine days? Working days?'

'Look, I don't know. All I know is that if he was seeing him four times in nine days it was on his business, not mine.'

Hanafi himself came to the door. Owen had thought he might not remember him, but he nodded in recognition and led him into the room with the piano. It was still there. Owen had half expected it not to be.

'How are you?' he asked.

Hanafi shrugged.

'Schneider says you're beginning to get back to work. That's good.'

Hanafi shrugged again.

'It is best to keep occupied.'

'Yes,' said Hanafi, without conviction. 'So they say.' He looked down at his hands and then up again. 'But what is the point?' he said. 'What is the point now? Everything I did, I did for her. She was my point. She gave my life meaning.'

'You will have to find other meanings,' said Owen gently.

'The only ones left for me now are the old ones,' said Hanafi despondently. 'The ones I wanted to get away from.'

'There are other meanings.'

'That is what we thought. She and I. We thought we could find them together. And if they weren't there, we thought we could build them. Together.'

He was no longer talking to Owen. He seemed to have forgotten him altogether, to be talking to himself.

'It was not just our lives that we were building, it was everyone's lives. We thought we would build a new society, a society with new meanings.' He made a little, hopeless gesture. 'But then we came up against society and found that it had already built its meanings and didn't want ours. Its meanings were like walls and held people apart. They held you in and if you tried to cross them they wouldn't let you. And if by any chance you did succeed in crossing them, then the walls closed behind you and locked you out. We tried to break them down but they were too strong for us. And in the end we had to settle for the old meanings. The

132

ones I had tried to get away from. And if it was hard for me, it was – well, impossibly hard for her.'

'You must not blame yourself.'

'Who should I blame, then?'

'I do not think,' said Owen, 'that in these things it is wise to look for blame.'

'Well,' said Hanafi doubtfully, 'you may be right. What was it that you wished to see me about?'

'It is a small thing,' said Owen, 'and I hate to trouble you at such a time. But it may be that you can help me. It is to do with some work I have.'

'Oh, yes?'

'It touches on Fricker Effendi and the time when he was at Minya.'

'Ah, Fricker Effendi!'

Hanafi's face brightened.

'You knew him, of course.'

'Of course!'

'And had lunch with him, I understand?'

'Yes, indeed.'

'I wonder – would you mind telling me what you talked about?'

'Talked about?'

'It was business, I presume?'

'Business? No.'

'I'm sorry, I thought –'

'Oh, I see. What was I doing in Minya on a working day, you mean?'

'Four working days. In such a short time.'

'I was there on business. But the business was not with Fricker Effendi. It was with the mudir.'

'The mudir?'

'Yes.'

'Schneider Effendi does not remember this business.'

'He wouldn't, it was with me. The mudir summoned me directly.'

'Four times?'

'Yes. He wanted me to carry messages for him to people here. And then I had to take back their replies. But then he

133

had questions and they needed further replies. So I was going into Minya a lot.'

'Without Schneider Effendi knowing?'

Hanafi shrugged.

'He does not need to know everything. He wouldn't have minded.'

'What was the subject of the messages?'

'That,' said Hanafi, with a touch of reproof, 'is for the mudir to say.'

'Of course. I ask only in connection with my work. They were not about ghaffirs, by any chance?'

'Ghaffirs?'

'Yes.'

'No,' said Hanafi, 'they were not about ghaffirs. Fricker Effendi asked me about ghaffirs,' he volunteered.

'He did?'

'Yes, but that was when I first met him. At the mudir's. They had been talking about ghaffirs, I think, and Fricker Effendi turned to me. But I know nothing about ghaffirs.'

'You did not talk about it at your lunches?'

'No.' Hanafi smiled. 'I think that for Fricker Effendi that was work, and he didn't want to talk about work. Neither did I, for that matter.'

'So what did you talk about?'

Hanafi's face lit up.

'Everything. Music, of course, and the time when he used to sing and Hilde used to play for him. But not just that. Ideas – everything! What they were talking about in Cairo, whether there would be war, and what changes it might bring. He said that in Cairo everyone was talking change. The politicians, the young effendis in the Ministries, the Ministers themselves! It was, he said, a ferment of ideas. And when he spoke, it was like – it was as if a hole had been opened in one of those walls, and suddenly I saw again what I had seen once before, when I went up to Cairo for the first time, and everything was possible.'

His eyes continued to shine for a moment; then they dulled.

'There was a time,' he said quietly, 'when I, too, believed

in change. I went to meetings, I distributed leaflets, marched in processions, shouted for Mustapha Kamil. And Hilde was part of it. She did not shout as I did, she did not march; but she shared in the excitement, she shared in the belief in change.'

He looked again at Owen.

'So what did we talk about? And what did we talk about when I took him home so that Hilde could listen too? Life,' he said. 'Life, that was what we talked about.'

His cheeks suddenly caved in.

Owen walked away from the house, thinking. This was a new side of Fricker that he was seeing and it was an unexpected one. Fricker, the bringer of sweetness and light? That pedant? That believer in systems and procedures, in lists of suggestions? That archetypal, as he had thought, apostle of Germanic efficiency?

But he could see how he would have appeared to the Hanafis: to Aziz a reminder of that bright new world he had once aspired to, and to Hilde a reminder of that life that had once, nearly, been hers.

They had thought they could take on the world. The world, unfortunately, was always likely to be a victor in such encounters.

The real problem, though, was that they had sought, as Hanafi had put it, to cross one of society's walls, and had paid the price. He found himself wondering whether it would be like that for Zeinab and him, if they, too, tried to cross the wall.

He didn't think it would. Not for him, at any rate. A man's place in this kind of expatriate society was defined by his work, and that would continue. Unless, of course, Kitchener had other ideas. But then, especially in the general uncertainty of war, there would be other work for him, if only in the Army.

But Zeinab?

Mahmoud had been visiting Old Mother Tayi.

'She didn't put the evil eye on you?'

Mahmoud looked at Owen uncertainly. He wasn't quite sure how to take this. If it was a joke, he wasn't sure he liked it.

'These people are very backward,' he said, 'but it isn't their fault.'

'Of course not.'

He explained how he had come to hear of her doubtful gift.

'That mamur,' said Mahmoud, 'he's another. For an educated man –'

'At least it shows he's close to the villagers,' said Owen.

Mahmoud wasn't sure about this, either. Was being close to the villagers a good thing if the villagers were backward and superstitious? He himself didn't feel close to them at all. He didn't know how to take the banter of the women, he could hardly believe the credulousness of the men and, although he wouldn't allow himself to say it, even to himself, he couldn't stand the squalor.

'Of course, she has a wider role in the village,' he said sternly. 'She helps as a midwife, she lays out the dead, advises about the prospects for the crops –'

He stopped. As a matter of fact, he wasn't too happy about this, either, in so far as it was an aspect of her soothsaying. Advice offered on rational grounds was obviously acceptable, but advice offered on the basis of a supposed ability to predict the future . . .

'What did she tell you?' asked Owen.

The door was opened this time not by Hanafi but by one of his brothers. Mahmoud asked if he could speak to the mother. The man disappeared. Again there was scurrying inside, and much muttering, and the feeling of there being many people. Then the mother came to the door.

'Well?' she said.

'I would like to speak with you.'

'You have spoken with me already.'

'And now I wish to speak with you again. And ask you some questions.'

'You have asked me questions before.'

'These are new ones; and they need answering.'

The mother hesitated. Someone called to her from inside. She shook her head impatiently and went on standing there.

Hanafi suddenly appeared beside her.

'Mother –'

She shook her head again, sharply, almost dismissively.

'Ask on, then,' she said to Mahmoud.

Mahmoud had been addressing her directly. Now, in the presence of her son, he put his questions through him, as custom prescribed.

'She bought some poison from Old Mother Tayi,' said Mahmoud. 'Ask her what for.'

'Mother –'

She silenced him with a gesture. Then she stood there, looking at Mahmoud. Suddenly she laughed.

'To kill the cats,' she said.

'What?' said Mahmoud, taken aback.

'To kill the cats,' she said impatiently. 'The cats that that woman brought to the house.'

'What is this?' Mahmoud said to Hanafi.

'There was a cat that Hilde fed,' said Hanafi.

'More than one,' said the old woman sharply. 'There was a plague of them.'

'Where are they now?' said Mahmoud, his eye travelling round the courtyard.

'Dead.'

There was a little silence. Then Mahmoud said:

'Mother, a cat is a small creature, and it does not take much to poison it. Did it take all the poison that you bought?'

'There were many cats.'

'How many?'

'How would I know?' retorted the woman. 'The place was infested with them.'

'Five?'

'Possibly.' She shrugged.

'I shall find out,' said Mahmoud. 'And then I shall ask you what you did with the rest of the poison.'

'And I shall tell you,' said the woman unexpectedly. 'I have it still.'

'Show me.'

'Very well.'

She went back into the house and returned a little later with something wrapped in sugar cane leaves.

'There!' she said triumphantly.

Mahmoud undid the leaves.

'I shall take this,' he said.

'Take it, then.' She smiled malignantly. 'The cats are all dead,' she said.

12

The sugar cane ran right down to the water. There was no jetty here or port area as there was in Minya because sand-banks came in close to the edge, but when they emerged from the sugar cane they found that the river bank had been cut away at that point and women were walking down into the shallows to fill their pots. When they had filled them, they put them on their heads and went gracefully back up to the village.

Mahmoud led Owen aside – it would be unmannerly to stand there watching the women – and they sat down high up on the river bank. It was late afternoon by now and the shadow of the sugar cane was beginning to creep across the water. The women would be going back to prepare the evening meal.

Mahmoud looked at his watch.

'She usually comes about now,' he said.

They sat on for a little while, studiously not looking at the women but hearing all the time their cheerful chatter. And then they heard fresh voices in the sugar cane and a moment later a new group of women came out on to the river bank. They did not go down into the water at once but sat down on the bank talking.

Mahmoud stood up and went down to them.

'Greetings, ladies!' he said courteously, if a little stiffly. Mahmoud was not good with women.

They knew it, of course.

'Greetings, Mahmoud!' they chorused back; but then one of them looked up at him mischievously and said: 'But, alas, you're not really interested in us, are you? You only want to talk to Fatima.'

Mahmoud blushed.

'I do indeed want to talk to Fatima,' he said. 'On business matters,' he added firmly.

'We know what sort of business that is!'

'That is not so!' said Mahmoud, blushing again.

'Don't tease him,' said one of the other women. 'Mahmoud is a married man.'

'What's your wife like, Mahmoud? Is she pretty?'

Mahmoud was plainly not sure how to answer the question; or, indeed, whether to. They all laughed mercilessly.

Taking pity, one of them stood up and Mahmoud led her hastily away up on to the bank where Owen was standing.

'Gracious, there are two of them! What skills the woman has!'

The group dissolved in laughter.

'This is Fatima,' Mahmoud said to Owen. 'She is the sister-in-law I spoke of.'

'You have spoken of me?' said the woman. She seemed pleased.

'To my friend only. And only because he, too, is looking into the death of the foreign woman.'

'They are more interested in her now that she is dead than when she was living,' said the woman, with a touch of acerbity.

'That may, unfortunately, be so.'

'I know you,' Fatima said to Owen. 'You came to the house before.'

'I did not see you then.'

'But I saw you!' said the woman, her eyes glinting.

There was no doubt, thought Owen, that the women were much freer in the provinces. Had she married into the family from down here? That might explain her relative independence.

'I have been talking to your mother,' said Mahmoud. The title was a general one which embraced mothers-in-law.

Fatima made a face.

'That must have been a pleasure for you,' she said.

'She has purchased poison. I asked her why.'

Fatima sobered.

140

'What did she say?' she asked.

'She said she had used it to kill cats.'

Fatima nodded.

'There were cats?'

'At first there was one, which Sitt Hilde was fond of. She used to feed it. Then others came.'

'And she poisoned them?'

Fatima nodded again.

'When? Before Sitt Hilde died or afterwards?'

'Afterwards. The men were very angry. They said it would make the Cat Woman come again.'

'Again?'

'The men think it was the Cat Woman who came for Sitt Hilde. But that is nonsense.'

'It certainly is!' said Mahmoud.

'I know it is,' said Fatima. 'For Sitt Hilde and the Cat Woman were friends.'

'Friends!'

'Our mother used to complain about Sitt Hilde feeding the cats in our yard. She said they would come into the house. So then Sitt Hilde took to feeding them outside the wall, at the edge of the sugar cane. And once when she was doing that I saw her talking to the Cat Woman.'

'Now, come, Fatima,' said Mahmoud. 'This cannot be.'

'I saw her!' said Fatima indignantly. 'They sat down together and talked.'

'Some other woman, perhaps?'

'No, the Cat Woman. Well, of course, there's no such person. But the Nubian woman they call the Cat Woman.'

'You saw her?'

'I certainly did. And afterwards I spoke with Sitt Hilde and taxed her with it. And she did not deny it but said: ''If that is where I must find my friends, if that is what it has come to, then so be it.'' She said she had met her before and that they had talked often. The Nubian woman had told her her story and it was a sad one. She had lost her child and another one wouldn't come, and her husband had beaten her. And one day when he was beating her, she had taken a knife and stabbed him. And then she had to run away and hide

141

in the sugar cane, and it was there now that she lived. And I said to Sitt Hilde: "Take care lest one day she stab you too." But Sitt Hilde said: "No, no, she will not stab me, for she is my friend."'

'I find this strange, Fatima,' said Mahmoud.

Fatima shrugged.

'Nevertheless, it is as I have said.'

'I do not doubt it. But still I find it strange. For how can two people so different be friends?'

'Perhaps,' said Fatima, 'they both liked cats!'

A water buffalo came nodding along through the shallows, a small boy behind it urging it on with a stick. When it came to the place where the bank was cut away, it climbed up out of the river and disappeared into the sugar cane.

The women chattering on the bank stood up, picked up their pots and went down into the water.

'Still at it, then, Fatima?' one of them called, as they came up on to the bank again. 'Which one are you going to take for a walk in the sugar cane? Tell me, and I'll take the other!'

'I think she'll take both,' said someone else. 'She's like that, you know.'

'Well, she'd better get on with it or else that husband of hers will be wondering why she's taking so long.'

'It's not her husband she ought to be worried about. It's that old bitch of a mother-in-law!'

As they were going back up the path through the sugar cane, keeping a decent distance behind Fatima, Owen said:

'Have you talked to the ghaffir here?'

'I don't think so. Why?'

'Is the ghaffir a man?'

Mahmoud looked at him cautiously.

'What else would he be?'

'A girl.'

'You are joking, yes?'

'No.'

Owen told him about the girl in the village he had passed through.

142

'But that is disgraceful!' cried Mahmoud.

'That is what I told them.'

'It is shaming!' fumed Mahmoud. 'It is backward. To treat their responsibilities so lightly!'

'We know that these things happen. People do not always choose the wisest man in the village for their ghaffir.'

'But to choose a girl!' said Mahmoud, shocked.

'They did not choose. Or so they said. That is what I find puzzling.'

'I find it hard to believe,' said Mahmoud. 'The village chooses a ghaffir from among its own members. That is the principle. Always.'

'But not in that village.'

Mahmoud frowned.

'There were, perhaps, circumstances special to the village.'

'That is what I wondered. And so I asked about the ghaffir here.'

'I have not seen him, but this I can tell you,' said Mahmoud. 'He won't be a woman!'

He stopped.

'As you shall see,' he said, striking off the path towards the houses.

'He'd better not be!' he said, his face set ominously.

They found the omda sitting on the ground in front of his house, surrounded by a group of his cronies. They were playing a game that looked to Owen rather like the English game of five stones.

'Greetings, Salah Hussein!' said Mahmoud.

'Greetings, Mahmoud. And to you, Effendi.'

'I come in search of the ghaffir,' said Mahmoud.

'Then you have found him,' said the omda, nodding in the direction of one of the men, an elderly, worried-looking man with hollow cheeks and a consumptive-sounding cough.

'You are the ghaffir?'

'I am.'

'That is a relief,' said Mahmoud. 'I feared for the moment that you might be a woman.'

143

This might have been meant as an insult and the man bridled.

'Why did you suppose that, Mahmoud?' asked the omda.

'Because my friend here met such a ghaffir in a village nearby.'

'Oh, that!' said the omda. The circle relaxed. 'That would be at Dejd.'

'It is a strange thing,' said Mahmoud. 'How did it come about?'

The omda shrugged.

'It just came about,' he said.

'It is not as it should be. For ghaffir one needs a man. As our friend here. For how can a slip of a girl be expected to fight off bad men if they come?'

The ghaffir looked even more worried.

'Besides,' said Owen, 'one needs as ghaffir a man who knows the ways of the village. As I am sure our friend here does. You come from this village, of course?' he said, turning to the man.

'Well, as a matter of fact . . .' began the ghaffir, looking at the omda anxiously.

'He comes from Bashawi,' said the omda.

He pointed across the sugar cane.

'Far, is that?'

'Far enough. A day's journey.'

'Ah, I see.'

Owen gave him some time. Then he said to the ghaffir:

'And how was it, then, that you came to be chosen by this village as its ghaffir?'

'Chosen?' said the man, looking puzzled.

'Repute,' said the omda quickly. 'We chose him by repute.'

'Yes,' said one of the other men helpfully, 'repute as a fighting man.'

The ghaffir looked aghast.

The next day, back at Minya, Owen went to see the mudir. He found him outside at his usual table. Although it was still early in the morning there were already several empty bottles under the table and his face was sweating. When Owen told

144

him about the girl ghaffir the veins on his forehead seemed to swell alarmingly.

'Girl?' he shouted. 'Girl?'

'That is so.'

'The useless sods! I'll have their balls for this! Hamid!' he shouted. 'Hamid!'

The mamur came running out of the house.

'Yes, boss?'

'Hear this: one of the ghaffirs out in the sugar cane is a girl!'

The mamur shrugged.

'They're a backward lot, boss.'

'Yes, but – a girl!'

'Perhaps they thought she could double up and do some other things for them at the same time?' suggested the mamur.

'She's about twelve,' said Owen.

'Hear that? Twelve! You pervert, Hamid!'

'Boss –'

'They're laughing at us! They're laughing at you, Hamid!'

'The bastards!' said the mamur automatically.

'They're laughing at me! Their mudir! Well, I'll bloody show them. *You'll* bloody show them. Get out there, Hamid, and sort it out!'

'Sort it out?'

'Yes. You can take the early truck.'

'But, boss –'

'Yes?'

'What do you mean, sort it out?'

'Tell them to get a new ghaffir.'

The mamur looked worried.

'But, boss, is that for me? Is that for you? I mean, isn't it interfering?'

'Of course it's interfering! If they pick a twelve-year-old girl, what the hell do they expect?'

'But, boss –'

The mamur looked very unhappy.

'What's the matter?'

'Boss, I don't like interfering. Is it a good idea?'

145

'Well, we've got to do something, haven't we? Now that the Effendi has pointed this out. So get out and do it!'

'Go over there?'

'That's right.'

'And tell them they've got to get a new ghaffir?'

'That's right.'

The mamur looked perturbed.

'Boss, I don't know that they'll listen to me.'

'Of course they'll listen to you! You're the mamur, aren't you?'

'Boss, I think it would be better if it came from you.'

'Well, it does come from me, doesn't it?'

'Yes, but I think it would be better if it came from you directly.'

'Well, I'm not bloody going over there myself, if that's what you're thinking. I've got things to do here.'

'Couldn't you send a message? Honestly, boss, it would be much better if it came from you. They would listen to you.'

The mudir reached a hand beneath the table, pulled up a bottle of beer, took a swig, and considered.

'You're the big man, boss, and I'm just a little one. They mightn't pay any attention to me.'

The mudir took another swig.

'You could be right,' he said. He sat there thinking. 'OK,' he said, 'I'll tell you what we'll do. I'll send a message *and* I'll send you.'

As he was going back into the town Owen saw the mamur walking glumly ahead of him. He quickened his pace and caught up.

'What's the matter, Hamid? You've been out there before!'

'Yes, I know,' said the mamur. 'But that was different.'

'How is it different?'

'It wasn't interfering. I mean, it was just a woman. And a foreign one at that. Now who cares about that? Nothing to do with anybody. I could just go in and do what I wanted. I wasn't interfering. But this!'

146

'For Christ's sake!' said Owen. 'It's only a matter of telling them to change a ghaffir!'

But the mamur continued to look glum.

'Look, I've been to the village myself. I've already spoken to the omda. They'll be expecting something like this.'

The mamur remained sunk in depression.

'He ought to have sent a message *first*,' he said. 'Send a message and then send me. He ought to have made sure it would be all right.'

'All right?' said Owen, puzzled.

'It's better if it comes from him. He knows them, after all.'

'Knows them? How does he know them?'

'Because he was out there, Effendi. Before me. Didn't you know that, Effendi? He was mamur out there for some years before he became mudir. He knows everybody. I don't mind telling you, Effendi, it's been a bit difficult taking over from him. In fact, I try to stay in Minya as much as I can. It's better that way.'

'You surprise me when you say he moved from mamur to mudir. That is a big step.'

'It is indeed, Effendi. The world was greatly surprised.'

'How did it come about?'

'It was the previous mudir, Effendi. He thought highly of him. "He's the only one down here with any brains," he used to say. And when he himself was moved away, he saw to it that our mamur became his successor. "Continuity is a great thing in office," he said. "That way we share the same interest and no one asks the wrong questions."'

'He said that?'

'It was the way he spoke, Effendi. And our mudir speaks in the same way.'

When they reached the waterfront they shook hands and the mamur climbed up into the truck. The driver had evidently completed his business in town and was waiting to go.

Owen had worked it out now. The truck served both as a company vehicle and as a general means of transport for those going to the factory. It came into Minya twice a day, in the morning and in the evening, carrying passengers and goods to and fro.

Its arrival, certainly in the morning, was timed to coincide with the arrival of the steamer from down river. The driver would pick up any packages there were for the sugar factory.

They would not be left lying for long. The truck would arrive just before the steamer and could depart immediately after.

He checked it that evening. The boat this time was from the south. The truck came bumping down to the end of the jetty just as it appeared round the bend. There were a few sacks and crates to be unloaded and just two of them were for the factory. The truck driver identified them and porters threw them up into the back of the truck. Then the truck drove off. It would be easy, thought Owen.

The truck hadn't been carrying many people this time. They climbed down and went up into the town. Owen looked for the mamur, but he was not among them.

13

He was not on the truck the next morning, either, when it came in. Owen asked after him, but the driver appeared to know nothing.

This time when the truck went back, Owen went with it. He sat in the cab with the driver but found it difficult to engage him in conversation. He wasn't sure if he was being guarded in his replies or whether he was just naturally uncommunicative.

After a while he settled back to enjoy the journey. Now he was getting used to the truck he found it quite agreeable. The countryside, the fellahin working in the fields close to the river, the tops of the sails behind the palm trees, the buffaloes working the water-wheels, went by so quickly. When you looked at things close to, it was disconcerting. Further away, though, they fell into place. It was like seeing things from a boat.

When they came to the sugar cane there was less to see, just the tall cane itself, stretching to the horizon, concealing the few villages until you were right on top of them, unless you happened to see a dovecote sticking out above the palms.

They were able to see the factory, though, some time before they got to it, partly because it was on a rise, partly because it was substantial enough for its roof to show above the cane. The driver swung down a track and came out into the factory compound.

There seemed to be trouble of some kind. Men were running about, Schneider was standing there cursing. The omda was there, and Mahmoud.

As Owen got down from the cab, Schneider was saying angrily:

'But I saw her, I tell you! She was in my office. Bending over my desk. Naked.'

'Naked?' said Mahmoud.

'Not a stitch. It took me aback, I can tell you. Seeing her there like that.'

'You weren't expecting her?'

'Expecting her? For Christ's sake! She had broken in. She was *stealing* something from me.'

'What was she stealing?'

'I don't know. I haven't had a chance to look yet. She had a paperweight in her hand.'

'A paperweight?'

'Yes. A big glass one. Like a ball. My wife gave it me. I keep it on my desk. Well, she'd picked it up. And then, well, she saw me and – and just ran.'

'Past you? You were in the doorway?'

'Well, I was so taken aback. She just pushed past me. And then she was off. Down the corridor and out into the yard. I ran after her, but then –'

'Yes?'

'Just as I got out into the yard, she jumped. Jumped clean over the wall.'

'Scrambled, perhaps.'

'Jumped. Look, I bloody saw it! Jumped. I never would have believed it. She went clean over the wall.'

'And then?'

'I ran to the gate. But by the time I'd done that, and got it open, she'd gone. Into the sugar cane, I imagine.'

'You didn't see her?'

'No. I shouted, but –' He shrugged his shoulders. 'Anyway, that's it. I sent for you. And a fat lot of good you've been!' he said bitterly.

Mahmoud disregarded him.

'Did any of you see her?' he said to the workmen.

They all looked away.

'For Christ's sake!' said Schneider. 'You must have seen her! Abu, you were right by the feed –?'

150

The man shook his head.

'Suleiman, surely you –'

But he, too, did not respond.

'Someone must have seen her!' said Schneider.

The men stood there woodenly.

'Look,' said Schneider. 'I didn't imagine this! Tariq? Hassan?' he appealed.

'Perhaps you'd better go and see if she had tried to take anything else,' said Mahmoud.

Schneider looked around for a moment, then shrugged and went inside.

The yard had filled up with people. Women, as well as men, had come out of the houses. They were standing there silently. But then, as Schneider went inside, a buzz of excited chatter broke out.

Among the women Owen thought he recognized Fatima, although it was difficult to tell, heavily veiled and wrapped up as she was. She was standing with a group of men and women: the Hanafi household, Owen imagined. An older woman was there too, the mother, presumably. Some of the men were talking angrily to her.

'It's your doing,' they were saying. 'You've brought her back!'

'She does what she wants,' said the old woman.

'You shouldn't have done it! Killed those cats!'

The old woman ignored them.

Owen felt a touch on his arm. It was Fatima.

'She came to our house, too,' she whispered.

'And spoke with you?'

'She spoke with no one. She just came into the house.'

'I do not understand.'

'She came into the house,' said Fatima, 'while we were eating our meal. The door was open.'

'But –?'

'She went to the Sitt's room and took a dress. No one saw her but I.'

'A dress? What sort of dress?'

151

Fatima shrugged.

'Just a dress,' she said. 'She had it over her arm. I saw her when she was leaving.'

The men were going back to work. A truck had been halfway through discharging its load. The men began to feed the conveyor belt again.

Owen heard them talking.

'Did you see her tits, then, Ibrahim?' one of them asked enviously.

'I did.'

'What were they like?'

'Colossal.'

The omda was standing nearby, talking to a group of villagers.

'She's always doing it!' the omda was complaining. 'It's got to stop!'

'What that woman needs is a good beating,' said the ghaffir.

'Are you going to give it her, then, Ja'affar?' asked someone.

'Me?' said the ghaffir, nervously. 'I don't fight women!'

'It's not a question of fighting –'

'Oh, yes, it is,' said the ghaffir. 'With that one, it is. She's a real wild one.'

'They say she's half cat,' said one of the villagers nervously.

'I don't think that's very likely,' objected the omda. 'I mean, how would it come about?'

'They say her mother mated with a leopard,' said the villager. 'They have leopards down there where she comes from, you know.'

'Well, all I can say is that her mother must have been a dirty bitch.'

'They say it jumped on her one day as she was going to the river.'

There was a little silence.

'Anyway, she needs a good beating,' said the ghaffir.

'I don't think it's a good idea to beat someone who's half leopard,' said someone uneasily.

'She isn't half leopard! That's a lot of nonsense!' said the omda angrily.

'The way she is,' said the ghaffir, 'it doesn't make much difference.'

Mahmoud came out of the office with Schneider. Schneider turned angrily away and went to his house. Mahmoud came across to Owen.

'Have you seen Hanafi?' he said.

Owen looked across to where the Hanafi household were standing.

'Isn't he there?'

'No. And Schneider doesn't know where he is, either.'

'Why do you want him?'

'He was seen talking to her this morning. Early. When the children were taking the goats out.'

'Her?'

'This woman. The Cat Woman. They say he's done it before.'

'She was up at the house afterwards.'

'The house?'

'The Hanafis' house. Fatima told me. She went in and took a dress.'

'A *dress*?' said Mahmoud.

Schneider came out on to the verandah with Mrs Schneider and they stood for a moment talking. Then Schneider came down the steps and went back to the factory. Mrs Schneider turned and saw Owen. She waved a hand.

'Coffee?' she called. 'Just made!'

She led him into the dining room, where a tray was standing on a low table. The house-boy came and cleared away the cups, and then brought fresh ones. Mrs Schneider waited until he had finished and then said quietly:

'What is all this about?'

'I don't know that it's *about* anything. It appears to be an attempted break-in, that's all.'

'Gerhardt says she was naked.'

'I wouldn't make too much of that. It's not uncommon

153

here. Thieves sometimes strip naked before breaking into a house. Then they grease their bodies. It makes them hard to hold if anyone catches them.'

'Yes, but – a woman!'

'It's usually children.'

Mrs Schneider paused for a moment and then nodded.

'I'm sure it's all right really,' she said. She laughed. 'He wouldn't have told me, otherwise, would he? It's just that – well, one wonders. One's on one's own so much down here that one doesn't always see things straight.'

She poured him some coffee.

'It's nice to have you here again. You and Mr el Zaki. One sees so few people. It's strange. We go on for years in our little enclave and nobody takes any notice of us; and then suddenly people are coming all the time. The world has remembered us.'

'I don't know I'm the world.'

'Oh, you are, you are. When you came the first time, it wasn't just you, it was the great world breaking in. Not just Cairo with all its rules and regulations and interfering bureaucracy, but the world outside Egypt, the Great Powers, Britain, Germany: their preoccupations, their wars. And you, with all that internment business, were the face on that.'

'It did not affect you, though?'

'No. Not directly. Switzerland is neutral. Even so, we were worried when we heard about the Government's plans for internment.'

'You need not have been. It was just Germans.'

'Not just Germans. Buried in one corner was a reference to suspicious aliens. Were we suspicious? I had not thought so, but suddenly I looked at us through the eyes of others and, yes, we were suspicious. We spoke German, didn't we? Gerhardt said it was important to stress that we were Swiss, neutral, and that all he was interested in was doing his job.

'Well, that was easy for him. All he *is* interested in is his job. But what about me? What was I interested in? Christ knows!

'We thought that in all the confusion people might not be

154

too concerned about making careful distinctions. Even the admirable Captain Owen! We thought he might be so busy, what with all the people to be interned, that he might not be able to *afford* to make careful distinctions. We were afraid that we might be taken away and put in some awful camp.

'Of course, if it was hard for us, it was worse for the Hanafis. She really was German.'

'They talked about it with you?'

'Yes. Hanafi came to see Gerhardt several times. They talked about it a lot and Gerhardt told me. They were terribly worried. Well, worried isn't the word for it. They just couldn't contemplate it, couldn't bear the thought. It would mean them being apart, and they had never been apart, not once, through all the hard times they'd had. They were in despair. She even came to see me.'

She grimaced.

'That "even". I feel guilty now. It ought not to have been "even". She ought to have been coming to see me anyway. I ought to have been going to see her. It was for me to take the initiative. But that awful house, that awful family!

'Well, I didn't go to see her. But then she came to see me. It took something like the prospect of internment to make her do that. She was proud. She didn't want to turn to me for help. She didn't want to turn to one of her own kind. Perhaps because she felt that they had rejected her.

'It was easier for her husband. He could go to Gerhardt and talk things over, he was used to doing that. They were close to each other, in that strange way that people who work together sometimes are. And Gerhardt would want to help. You mustn't mind him; his bark is worse than his bite. He wanted to help Hanafi, but it wasn't easy to see how. He was worried about us ourselves, about the war in general. The world seems so big when it breaks in on you. It fills the sky.

'And so it must have been hard for her to come to me. It ought not to have been so hard. I feel ashamed. I knew what it was like for her in that house. I ought to have made things easier. Or at least tried to. Long before.

'It was only when she was desperate that she came to me.

155

When she thought it was going to end. Even life in that dreadful house seemed preferable to it all coming to an end, their togetherness, which was all they had.

'And, of course, when she came to me, I couldn't help her. She wanted reassurance, and what could I give her? She said that surely since she was married to an Egyptian, she counted as Egyptian, that her German nationality didn't count. I asked her if she was registered with the German Consulate. What an awful, crass thing to say when a woman comes to you desperate for help.'

She was crying now.

'I am sorry,' she said, pulling herself together. 'Sorry.'

She broke down again.

The mamur had been in the village that morning, the omda said, hanging around and drinking tea, as if he was waiting for someone. But then he had disappeared. 'Where to?' asked Owen. The omda couldn't say.

Owen tried a number of other people, with the same result. Then he went up to the factory and questioned the drivers. They all agreed that he had come to the village the previous evening and spent the night there but where he was now they couldn't say.

He checked the trucks. They could all be accounted for. The mamur wasn't with or on any of them.

Owen found this hard to believe. Surely he would not have left the village on foot! Not in this heat, and among the sugar cane?

But it appeared he had. He could only have gone to a village. Owen spent the afternoon eliminating these, some by talking to people, others by actually visiting them. In one case he borrowed a donkey, in two others he walked. It was extremely hot going anywhere in the sugar cane and by the end of the afternoon he was like a limp rag.

Well before the time of the truck's departure for Minya he was waiting in the compound. The truck was there but the driver wasn't. He didn't come until just before the truck was due to depart; but when he came, the mamur was with him.

He seemed much more at ease than when Owen had last seen him; cheerful, even.

'Hello, Effendi. What brings you out to a dump like this?'

'The same thing as you, perhaps.'

'No, I don't think so,' the mamur said easily.

'But you have been here on the mudir's business?'

'Oh, yes.'

'And have been successful?'

'Yes.' The mamur seemed to have no doubts now. 'You needn't worry, Effendi. The girl will be replaced. What a daft thing to do, to put in someone like that, where everyone can see! These people have no sense.'

'These people?'

'That's right.'

The mamur stood aside to let Owen climb up into the cab. Then he went to the back of the truck and got in with the other passengers.

The next morning Owen went to see the mudir. He found him in his usual place, sitting outside in the yard under the thatched awning. Although it was still early in the morning there was a bottle open on the table in front of him and beneath the table there were several more, standing in a bucket of ice.

'Hello, Effendi!' he said hospitably. 'Come and sit down. This heat! It's building up already.'

He put a bottle on the table before Owen.

'Well,' he said, 'that's all sorted out now. Hamid's had a word with them. There'll be a different ghaffir in place by this evening. Putting a girl there! When there are effendis about. Damned stupid!'

'But what if there weren't effendis about?'

'Well . . .'

'How many more are there?' said Owen. 'And what does it tell us about these splendid systems of yours?'

'Fricker Effendi –' began the mudir.

'Yes, yes, I know. But they're plainly not working. Not if powerful new service rifles can get handed over to twelve-year-old girls.'

The mudir took a long, deliberate drink. Although he had already drunk quite a lot, the eyes were still sober. They were watching Owen carefully, calculating.

Suddenly he smiled.

He put the bottle down and spread his hands, palms upwards, on the table.

'All right, Effendi,' he said, 'it's bad. I've got to admit that. But it's not as bad as you think. Look, Effendi, you're a man of experience. You've been out in the world, not like these little pricks from the Ministry. You know that things are a bit different down here in the provinces. It's all very well dreaming up something in Cairo, but when you've got to make it work in a place like Minya, it's a bit different.

'I'll be frank with you, Effendi. We've had to stretch Fricker Effendi's systems a bit occasionally. And where there's been stretching, well, perhaps one or two things have slipped through. But I think I know where it's gone wrong, Effendi. And what I'm wondering is this: could you just leave it to me? I know it's a lot to ask, but you're a man of experience, Effendi, and you know that it's sometimes best to let those on the spot sort things out. Leave it to me and I won't let you down. I'll find out where the system's gone wrong and put it right. I'm sorry about the girl. That was just a mistake. But mistakes happen in all systems, don't they?'

'They do; but it's a question of how often they happen.'

'Well . . .'

'Two hundred times, for instance?'

'Two hundred – ? No, no. Look, Effendi, you've got it all wrong. Believe me. Two hundred? No. One or two at the most. You've got it all wrong, Effendi. It's not like that at all. Look, I'm sorry about the girl. It's my fault, I admit it. My mind's been on other things lately. Things have been a bit tricky, and it must have slipped through. But it's just one case, Effendi. One case!'

'There aren't any other cases? Of other strange appointments? Of people being chosen from outside the village? Of people not being chosen at all but just drafted in from somewhere else?'

The mudir's hand felt below the table and gripped on a

bottle. He thought better of it and let it go. By the time he had straightened up again, though, he had recovered his composure.

He took his time about replying.

Then the big smile reappeared and the hands spread out upon the table.

'Effendi,' he said, 'I can see I'm going to have to do better. You're quite right. About there being mistakes, that is. Not about the two hundred – that's all nonsense, you're barking up the wrong tree there. But about there being mistakes. The fact is, things have been a bit tricky here lately. And mistakes have been made. But I'll put them right, Effendi, I promise you that.'

He picked up another bottle, wiped the top with his hand and took a long drink. Then he put it back in the bucket.

'But that's not going to be good enough for you, Effendi, is it? Not this time.'

He leaned forward, and suddenly he seemed quite formidable.

'This time you'll want to be sure. You'll want to see for yourself that things have been put right, won't you? And so you shall.

'Effendi, what I would like to propose is this: give me a day or two to put things right. And then you can go and see for yourself. My mamur will take you round. You can go to every village, if you want. You're worried about the ghaffirs? Right. You can go round and check every one. Personally. You'll see for yourself that every village has got a proper ghaffir and every ghaffir has got a proper gun. Not a gun will be missing. You'll be able to see for yourself. Now, Effendi –' the hands spread out again – 'what could be fairer than that? See for yourself. That's my offer.'

'All right,' said Owen. 'I'll take you up on that.'

14

When Owen got back to Cairo he went straight to his apartment. Zeinab wasn't there, nor had she left a note. He changed and went to his office. In his absence, brief though it had been, the pile of lists on his desk had grown to mountain-like proportions, and Nikos said that wasn't the half of it. For the last few days McPhee had been methodically working through the lists taking people into internment. He also said that there had been several calls from Cunningham, the Finance Adviser, and from Cavendish. Owen didn't like the sound of either of these and decided not to reply. Instead, he made a call of his own, to McKitterick, suggesting that they meet at lunch-time in the Sporting Club.

McKitterick came eagerly across the bar room to greet him.

'How have you been getting on?' he said.

His face seemed thinner and tauter. Owen guessed that the strain was getting to him.

'Oh, making progress, making progress,' he said. 'What'll you have?'

He took the drinks to a table in the corner.

'I'm beginning to get a picture of the people down there,' he said. 'But it would be helpful if you could fill me in with some of the background details.'

'Of course.'

'The mudir, for a start. Promoted from district mamur. Is that usual?'

'No, but he was highly recommended.'

'Who by?'

'The previous mudir, I think.'

'Who had himself moved from being mamur for that district.'

'Had he? I didn't know that.' McKitterick looked at Owen. 'That's not good, is it?'

'Well, it means that no one new has had a look at that district for quite a long time. A district where there appears to be a lot of brigand activity.'

McKitterick nodded, accepting.

'You think there have been abuses?' he asked.

'Possibly. What can you tell me about the previous mudir? The one before the present one.'

'Faruq Rahim? Well, very able. Unusually so. He didn't stay there long but was soon promoted. To Governor at Suez, which is really quite an important job. I think they had in mind a particular project they wanted him to work on. In fact, he didn't stay there long, either. He was soon promoted again.'

'What to?'

'They took him into the Ministry. Very unusual, that.'

'So where is he now?'

'Here.'

'Here? Here in the Ministry?'

'That's right. He's an Under-Secretary now.'

There was a letter waiting for him when he got back to his office. It was postmarked Alexandria and addressed in a neat, old-fashioned hand which he recognized.

Dear Captain Owen, it read:

I promised I would write to you again when I had gathered my thoughts. I cannot say that I have gathered them very successfully. At my age thoughts seem to ramble rather than gather! But at any rate I have thought of a few things to tell you. I am also enclosing a letter, the last one Hilde wrote to me. I thought it better that you read it for yourself, so that you can form your own judgement, rather than relying on my reduction of it. When you have read it, would you please return it to me? Her letters are all that I now

161

have of Hilde and I would wish to retain them. They bring her back to me, almost better than my own memories, which become, I am afraid, increasingly unreliable.

He found the letter behind her own. It was written on cheap, thin, blue paper and in several places the ink had smudged from the perspiration from her hand as she wrote.

Dear Mrs Pfarrer,
How nice to get your letter and to be reminded of that lovely cool breeze along the Rue de France! No cool breeze here, I'm afraid: each day this week, when I have gone out into the yard, I have found a bird lying there gasping. I move them into the shade and try water and sometimes it works. The Hanafis watch me, baffled.

The heat here is intense. It affects even the piano. I put bowls of water about the room but the water evaporates almost before my eyes. The sound is no longer true. Either that, or my playing is no longer true. I fear that may be so. The heat affects everything.

But perhaps it is not the heat.

You ask how things are. No better; perhaps no worse. We are desperate to get away. Aziz scans the appointments columns all the time. He says if we could only get away, get back to the city, things would be better. I am not so sure. His family would follow us. They are like an incubus. Or is it a succubus? Anyway, they suck you dry.

Aziz says that in the city they would drop into the background. They would still be living with us – he cannot imagine a life without that – but they would loom less large because there would be other things. Here there is nothing. The family is all round us, it is all there is. If I try to get away, to walk down to the river, for instance, on my own, someone is always sure to tell them and then the mother comes and upbraids me. It is not seemly, it is not proper. I disgrace my husband.

Whatever I do is wrong. It saps me, this continuous

162

carping. It saps Aziz, too, and in some ways it is worse for him, for he is torn as well as sapped, torn between duty to them and love for me.

That love is very real, Mrs Pfarrer. You were the one who always believed in it and you can still believe in it. It is all that keeps me alive. It is all, I think, that keeps Aziz alive. Sometimes he gets very depressed, when there is no response, for instance, to another of his countless applications for jobs. He is forever seeking a way of getting us out of here; he would do anything to get us out. He has tried all sorts of things but nothing ever seems to come of them. I sometimes feel we will be trapped here forever in this ghastly house in the sugar cane.

But perhaps we may not be. News of the great world sometimes trickles through to us even here and it appears that huge changes are happening in the world outside. There is even talk of war! How that could help us, we don't know. Perhaps it is just that, unable to change life for ourselves, our only hope is for life to change around us.

But what a thing it is to hope for war as a way out of one's difficulties!

He read on, and then turned back to the original letter. It concluded:

So you see, Captain Owen, perhaps I was wrong in my original letter to you to emphasize her depression. There is certainly depression here but, on re-reading this, surely there is also hope? At least there is vivacity – the vivacity I have always associated with her ever since she was a little girl. And while there is that, surely talk – as I fear I did – of suicide is premature.

Owen folded the letter and put it in an envelope to send to Mahmoud. Then, however, he changed his mind and put it in his pocket, intending to take it home and show it to Zeinab that evening.

She didn't get in till late and embraced him perfunctorily. She did not say where she had been, nor did she ask him about Minya. Instead she went into the bedroom. When he went in a little later he found her already in bed, not trying to sleep but staring at the ceiling.

'Is there anything wrong?' he asked.

'No,' she said. 'Why should there be?'

He gave her the letter to read. She glanced over it and then handed it back to him without comment.

He was a little surprised. She had seemed to have taken a particular interest in Hilde Langer.

'Are you all right?' he said again.

'Yes.'

She turned on to her side, away from him.

The next day, Owen went to see Fricker. The camp was bigger than before – there were more tents – and more crowded. There was an extra bed in Fricker's tent and the packing cases which had served as side-tables had been removed. The heat inside the tent was terrific.

'This is not good,' said Owen.

Fricker made a little resigned gesture.

'It is no worse than one should expect,' he said. 'I have suffered worse on my tours of inspection. I am not ill-treated. The food is not good, but it is sufficient. It is just –' he hesitated – 'that I miss my work. There is nothing to do; ever. I had not realized that work was so important to me. That it made up such a big part of me.' He shrugged. 'Well, enough. What can I do for you?'

'I come as a colleague,' said Owen, 'seeking a colleague's advice.'

'Well,' said Fricker. He seemed pleased. He drew himself together and bowed slightly. 'If I can help, I would be glad to do so.'

'It concerns the issue we spoke about before: the missing guns.'

'I cannot explain that,' said Fricker. 'I have thought about it a great deal. Yes, a great deal. I cannot understand it. The system should not have allowed it.'

164

'I think the system may have been perverted.'

'Well, that is possible,' said Fricker doubtfully. 'But –'

'Perhaps it is not the system that we should be looking at but the people.'

'Well, yes,' said Fricker, cheering up. 'People are very unreliable.'

'In that – possible – connection, I would like to ask you about some of the people you met down there. The mudir, for a start.'

'I have no reason to think him dishonest. Perhaps a trifle –' Fricker thought hard to find the word – '*rascally*. Is that right? Yes, rascally. But that was just an impression.'

'You got on with him all right?'

'Not at first. At first he was hostile, yes? He thought I was . . .' Fricker considered. 'Another prick from Cairo? Yes?'

'Very likely, yes.'

'He did not think much of the changes I wished to make. "Ghaffirs are stupid bastards," he said. "You won't get anything out of them. It's not a system you want, it's a miracle." So I went ahead without him. Then one day, to my surprise, he called me in and said: "Tell me about this system again." And after that he was quite different. Very supportive, very intelligent, even – he made some excellent suggestions. I think the turning point was when it became clear that the Ministry was likely to back my proposal to arm the ghaffirs properly. He saw then that we were serious, that we meant business.'

'That was when he began to take an interest?'

'That is so, yes. And afterwards I had no complaints about him at all. As I say, he was constructive and helpful, unusually so for a provincial mudir. A little loose on systems and procedure, perhaps, but –'

'He knew the area well, of course. He had been mamur out in the sugar cane before he became mudir. As had the previous mudir before him.'

'So I believe.'

'Did you know the previous mudir?'

'Faruq Rahim? No, the change had occurred before my time. I did meet him later, as a matter of fact. During one of my earlier postings. It was in the Suez area. He was the Governor there.'

'That was at the time of the wireless station project?'

'Yes. It was why I was posted there, I think. The contractors were going to be German – that is, if the project was approved – and, of course, I speak German. It was my first real posting. I was very honoured. Yes, pleased and honoured.'

'Sadly, the project came to nothing, I gather?'

'There were political considerations, so I understand. It was all, of course, far above my head.'

'Did you come across him later? When he was in the Ministry?'

'Oh, yes, sometimes. But, of course, he was far senior to me.'

'Did you talk to him about the ghaffirs?'

'Yes, I did, as a matter of fact. You see, he was one of the few senior people of the Ministry who had served in the provinces, who actually knew about ghaffirs and could understand the points I was making.'

'He supported the plan?'

'Oh, yes, very definitely. He said it was just what was needed.'

Owen asked him some technical questions about procedures and then thanked him and got up to leave. Fricker walked with him to the gate.

'I have been thinking about this a lot,' he said.

'Well, I wouldn't make too much of it. These things are bound to happen with any system.'

Fricker seemed surprised.

'You think so?' he said doubtfully.

As they approached the gates, he said:

'I do not think about it all the time. Much of the time I think about Hilde.'

'Sad,' said Owen.

'Yes. It, too, I cannot understand. Why would anybody . . . ?'

'I know. It is hard to imagine.'

'I think about Hilde a lot,' he said again.

166

'What exactly was your relationship with her?'

'My relationship?'

'You were not, by any chance, having an *affaire* with her?'

Fricker stopped in his tracks.

'I?' he said. 'I? Oh, no!' He was covered in confusion. 'Not I. No. I am not like that. Just music. Just music together, that was all. As in the old days. She wanted it. She wanted, I think, to go back to those days. And I, too, when she played and I sang, I thought how nice it would be.'

He looked at Owen.

'They wanted to get away, you know. Aziz spoke to me about it often. And I said I would try to help them. I would see if there was some job in the Ministry, or even outside the Ministry, but in Cairo. They wanted to come back to Cairo. And I thought, too, how nice that would be. We could play and make much music together again. But an *affaire* – oh, no! I am not like that, nor was she. And, besides, they loved each other. It was for her that he wanted to get away. But both together. Always together. That is what they wanted to be. That is good. I wish, sometimes, that I, too, had . . .'

He shook his head.

'But I am not like that,' he said. 'I have never married. I make my life by myself. But they – always together. They had to be together.'

'You have returned to civilization then?' said Kattim, smiling.

Owen had rung the Ministry of Finance and asked if he could talk to him privately, and the Egyptian had suggested a café on the Midan Nasriya.

They shook hands.

'Oh, I returned some time ago. In fact, I have been down there again since!'

'Indefatigable,' murmured Kattim.

He dropped into the chair opposite Owen.

'And have your visits proved fruitful?' he asked.

'Oh, yes, I think so. I think I am beginning to understand that end of it now. So now I am turning to this end. As, in fact, you advised me in the first place.'

167

Kattim spread his hands deprecatingly.

'Can I ask you something? You didn't stay at Minya very long. You just looked at the books and then off you went. Why was that?'

'I just can't bear the provinces!' said Kattim, laughing.

'So you said, I remember. But is that true?'

'It certainly is! Hot, sweaty, dirty and so, so primitive!'

'But you also told me that you yourself are a man from the provinces.'

'And the sooner I could get away from them, the better.'

'I think you said that too. But you know, despite what you say, I think you still have a soft spot for the provinces.'

'Surely not!' said Kattim, aghast.

'Oh, I think you do. In fact, I think that was partly the reason why you left. You didn't like to see the provinces taking all the blame.'

'You make me sound very charitable.' He was silent for a moment. 'Well, not all of it. Though some of it, certainly.'

'You felt your colleagues in the Ministry of the Interior were setting the mudir up.'

'Not entirely undeservedly.'

'No, but not entirely fairly, either. I think you saw at once that there could be no crime locally without a complementary crime at the Ministry – that it was not a question of either but of both.'

'Perhaps.'

The waiter put two cups on the table and poured them coffee.

'Tell me,' said Owen, 'what did you do when you got back to Cairo?'

'I put in a report critical of the Ministry of the Interior's internal processes.'

'And that was all?'

'It's quite a lot, actually,' said Kattim defensively. 'With another Ministry, that's about as far as you can go.'

'In fact, you went further,' said Owen. 'You tipped me off. I didn't quite understand the tip at the time, but I think I do now.'

168

Kattim smiled.

'The way it was worked was this,' said Owen. 'As you suspected, there were two requisition notes and also two consignment notes. The first requisition note was for eight hundred and fifty guns; but then the mudir sent in another one for one thousand and fifty guns. It was the second one that was worked to initially within the Ministry, the one which triggered a consignment note and a delivery to the boat that was going to transport the guns.

'The guns, one thousand and fifty of them, were duly delivered at Minya. But then the consignment note for one thousand and fifty guns, which had gone with them, was somehow lost and another substituted in its place. That second note, for eight hundred and fifty guns, not one thousand and fifty, was, of course, consistent with all the paperwork at the Minya end. It made it seem that there was nothing that they had to explain.

'Now I think that when you saw the books you worked out that it must be something like that and saw no reason why you should hang around any longer. Am I right?'

'Quite possibly,' said Kattim. 'What happened to the guns?' he asked.

'I think they were split up on the jetty, probably by the mudir's clerk Abdul, and two hundred were carried off at once, almost certainly in a truck from the sugar factory, while the rest were taken up to the police station.'

Kattim nodded.

Owen took a sip from his cup, then put the cup down.

'There are, though, two things that puzzle me. The first is this. You are a responsible, diligent official of the Ministry of Finance. You saw that a crime had been committed and you also, I think, saw how it had been done. And yet all you did, when you got back to Cairo, was to write a report criticizing the Ministry's procedures!'

'I have explained. I did, in fact, do quite a lot. The fact that it was another Ministry –'

'No, I don't think so. Or, at least, I don't think that was all of it. I think you thought that the Ministry itself might have had a hand in it. You thought that there might be some

169

political agenda here, a Nationalist one. And so you – a good Nationalist yourself, no doubt – decided to hold back.'

For a little while Kattim said nothing. Then he smiled.

'Something like that, no doubt,' he said. 'And the second thing?'

'Who the two hundred guns went to,' said Owen.

When Owen got back to the apartment, Zeinab was out on the balcony, looking into space. She hardly registered his presence when he sat down beside her.

'What is the matter?' he said.

'Nothing is the matter.'

'Something *is* the matter.'

At last she told him. While he had been away, she had visited one of her cousins, the Princess Fawzi. They were not especially close but Zeinab quite enjoyed her cousin's coffee mornings, when she picked up the latest Cairo gossip. That morning, though, she had sensed something in the air. Her cousin had seemed distant. And not just her cousin. The other people there, too, whom Zeinab normally got on with, had been, well, not exactly rude but somehow unwelcoming. She had had the feeling that she was being given – she looked at Owen to check the English – 'the cold shoulder, yes?' Not one to accept this, Zeinab, before she left, had pulled her cousin aside and demanded to know what was the matter.

After much humming and hawing, the Princess had said that it was her marriage.

'Marriage?' said Zeinab, astonished.

'If it's not true, I'm glad to hear it,' said Fawzi.

'What marriage?' said Zeinab.

'Yours, with that Englishman.'

Zeinab had started to say that there was no question of any such marriage, but then had stopped.

Instead, she said:

'People have known about this for ages. Why are they suddenly getting excited now?'

'An *affaire* was one thing. Marriage is another.'

'But –'

170

'Especially now. Now that the Turks are going to come in and throw the British out.'

'They're frightened, is that it?' said Zeinab, beginning to fire up.

'No. It's that they're beginning to take sides. After all, the Ottomans are our own people.'

'I marry whom I like!' said Zeinab, through clenched teeth.

'Why don't you like a good Egyptian, Zeinab? Is there something strange with you? Perverse?'

Zeinab by this time was getting very angry.

'If that's how you feel –!' she had said, and left.

'It's not how I feel, Zeinab,' her cousin called after her. 'It's how people feel.'

Zeinab had still been seething when she got home, but then a certain reaction had set in. *Did* people feel like that?

Over the next day or two she had sounded people out. In too many cases, unfortunately, it appeared that they did.

Even her musician and artist friends.

'You would have thought that they –' she said incredulously.

Cairo had somehow become different, she said. It was the war. It was giving everything a shake, deepening old fault lines. And suddenly it was becoming important to be on the right side of fault lines which in the past you had danced carelessly over.

Owen was shocked. Of course it did not come as a surprise to him. He had, he realized, been thinking about precisely this for some time, not just since he had become involved in the case of Hilde Langer, but certainly more acutely since then. He had thought, vaguely, that it would be worse for women; even that it might be hard for Zeinab. But somehow it had not really come home to him. Now it did.

He put his arms round her and tried to reassure her. She merely shrugged and turned away. Later, she got up and went into the bedroom.

But then she came out again and asked him if he still had Hilde Langer's letter. He had been keeping it, knowing that he would soon be going down to Minya again, when he could give it to Mahmoud personally. He found it and gave it to her. She read it through again, slowly and carefully this time. Then she handed it back.

'It won't be like that with me,' she said. 'I shall fight.'

15

Owen couldn't settle to anything the next morning. He found himself thinking about Zeinab all the time. Mid-way through the morning he received a message from Nuri Pasha, Zeinab's father. It asked him to come and see him as soon as he could. Owen guessed that it was about Zeinab and went at once.

It was not that at all; at least, not in the way he had imagined.

'My dear boy,' said Nuri, as soon as they had settled themselves together on the huge divan in the mandar'ah. 'I felt I really should have a word with you about this monstrous idea of yours – to go and fight in the war. It is making Zeinab most unhappy. I must say, I find it more than a little surprising myself. I thought you had outgrown such nonsense. Young men, I know, are always wanting to go and fight wars. They feel a need to prove their manhood. But you, my dear fellow, surely have no need, at this stage in your life, to prove that? Fighting is best left to people you employ for the purpose: the Sudanese, for instance. Certainly someone else.'

In a way, Owen was relieved. He had been afraid that Nuri, aware of the pressures on Zeinab, might have been about to ask him to back off from their relationship, at least until things had become clearer, and he was not at all sure how he was going to reply. Nuri, though, was evidently not so up-to-date.

'I remember, dear boy,' he said now, reminiscing, 'when I was your age, all hot to go and fight the Bulgars. My mistress at the time – it was Zeinab's mother, a very intelligent, strong-minded woman – said to me: "Nuri, is this wise? If you will not think of me, think of your country. It needs such talent as yours. At home."

'And, do you know, dear boy, on reflection I saw that she was right. Women are more realistic than we are. They see these things more clearly. We should trust their judgement more. And so, my dear fellow, I urge you: do listen to Zeinab on this. She is very clear-sighted on such things.'

'She is, Nuri. However . . .'

'And then there is another thing,' said Nuri, getting into his stride. 'Zeinab loves you, dear boy, and I, too, am very fond of you. I would be very glad to have you as my son-in-law. That is, if you were richer. I have brought up Zeinab to have expensive tastes –'

'You have, Nuri, you have.'

'– which even I am sometimes unable to provide for. What chance is there of your doing that on your present pay? Your career, dear boy – I hope you don't mind me saying so – languishes. War is an opportunity to improve matters.

'When all the other young men went away to fight, on the occasion I spoke of, they left gaps at Court which I was able to take advantage of. I was able to establish myself in the Khedive's favour and have never looked back. Let me urge you, dear boy, to seize this opportunity.'

Owen, relieved, promised to consider Nuri's wise words ('I speak as a father, dear boy . . .') and they lay on the divan, sipping sherbet and chatting, for some time.

Nuri Pasha had had a long, distinguished – not untarnished but always distinguished – political career which he hoped was not yet over. He had at one time been one of the Khedive's Ministers, until an unfortunate decision – he had backed the wrong horse: the British – had brought his ministerial career to an abrupt end. Ever since, hoping against hope, he had kept himself au fait with the political currents that ebbed and flowed around the Khedive's office. He was a mine of information about those who aspired to power, particularly information which might be used to discredit them. His contacts ran far and wide; and Owen, as he was lying there, suddenly had an idea.

'I wonder, Nuri,' he said, 'if in your peregrinations through

174

the corridors of power, you have ever come across a man named Faruq Rahim?'

'Faruq Rahim? I do not think so.'

'He is in one of the Ministries – Interior.'

'Ah!' Nuri thought. 'I have him now. But, dear fellow, if he is in the corridors of power, it is only as an office-boy!'

'I know, Nuri, by your standards –'

'He has turned out to be,' said Nuri, 'a great disappointment.'

'Why is he a disappointment, Nuri?'

'Because people had such great hopes of him. I remember talking to Ismail Ifqat Bey once – that was when Ismail was still a Minister – and him being very excited about a young man he'd found whom he thought would do excellently for a certain job. It may surprise you, dear boy, to know that Ministers are always on the look-out for bright young men. Well, Ismail thought he had found one.

'What he needed was someone capable who had had experience of work in the provinces. Well, of course, capability and provinces don't normally go together and he'd been having difficulties finding someone. And now here was someone who seemed to fit the bill in every way.

'The job was something to do with cable or wireless stations. At least, it wasn't directly to do with that, but the Ministry wanted someone locally who would facilitate the project – you know, someone who would know when to turn a blind eye. There was a political aspect to the scheme, you see. It was a German idea; they wanted to build a chain of such stations going all the way down the coast to German East Africa, and the Ministry supported it because they saw it as one in the eye for the British.

'Well, of course, when the British found out, they blocked it and the scheme came to an end. Faruq Rahim, though, had done enough to impress his superiors and so they promoted him into the Ministry. But then, dear boy, do you know what they found?'

Nuri paused dramatically.

'No?'

'They found he was not interested at all!'

175

'Not in promotion?'

'No, no, no. He was interested in promotion all right. But in politics. He wasn't interested in politics. It will come as no surprise to you, dear boy, that the people at the top of the Ministry were heavily Nationalist. That, of course, was how they had seen the wireless stations – as a means of striking a political blow at the British. They had taken it for granted that he had understood that and shared their views.

'It was only afterwards, after they had promoted him into the Ministry, that they found out. He was not at all interested in politics but only in money-making. There were rumours of over-close relationships with contractors, bribes, that sort of thing. Well, they didn't mind about the bribes, but the lack of political interest was quite another thing.'

'Nuri, are you sure about this? His lack of political interest? I must say, you surprise me.'

'Quite sure, dear boy. It brought his career to an end.'

'Nuri, this is important. I am investigating, you see, a certain incident in the provinces in which I think he may have been intimately involved, and I need to know if there is any likelihood that his actions were politically motivated.'

'No likelihood at all, dear boy. As I say, he has been a great disappointment.'

McPhee stuck his head round the door, then came right into the room.

'Gareth.'

Owen sat up. McPhee did not normally call him by his Christian name. This must be serious.

'Great news, Gareth. They've accepted me.'

'Accepted – ?'

'For the Army. I leave in a fortnight.'

'But he's too old! And he's halfway round the bend! He's –'

'He is,' agreed Zeinab, who thought that anyone who volunteered for the Army, particularly in war-time, was halfway round the bend.

'It's ridiculous!'

176

'It is,' she said happily, putting her arm around him.

'I must say, it makes one consider one's own position, though.'

'What?!' said Zeinab, withdrawing her arm.

'Well, you know. A man like that! When one has so much more to offer oneself.'

'But this man is a lunatic. You've said so yourself.'

'He is. But . . . but perhaps not altogether. Not in wanting to do his bit.'

'Cannot he do – what was that you said? – "his bit" outside the Army? Where he is?'

'It's not the same.'

'No, it is not. The man is evidently afflicted. One of the blessed of God. That being so, when he is "doing his bit" in normal life, he is obviously not doing it very well. He will do better off in the Army where it is not noticed.'

'It's not quite like that.'

'I would have said it was. Everyone knows that you send your weakest son. And if you don't want to do that, you pay some simpleton to go instead. That is why the Army is full of simpletons.'

'No, no, you haven't quite –'

'It is best if this man goes and you don't.'

Owen was silent.

This infuriated Zeinab, who knew it meant that she was not carrying him with her.

'Well, go, then! Go and get yourself killed! What is it to me? You're just a stupid Englishman!'

Faruq Rahim was in his mid-forties and was wearing a gold bracelet. That was the first thing that Owen noticed about him. It wasn't usual for under-secretaries to wear gold bracelets.

There were other things. His suit was well cut, certainly better cut than Owen's, better, Owen thought, even than Kitchener's. The shirt was good, too. Egypt was a cotton country and there were very good shirts to be obtained in Cairo. This one was silk.

He came forward to greet Owen with hand outstretched.

'I don't think we've met,' he said. 'Strange, isn't it? In a small place like Cairo.'

'My work doesn't usually bring me into the Ministry,' said Owen. 'And I daresay you're kept pretty busy.'

'Well, yes. Especially at the present time.'

'And short-staffed.'

'That, too,' Faruq Rahim agreed.

'I am afraid I have to accept some responsibility there – taking so many of them into internment.'

'The Germans, yes.'

'Of course, it makes space for Egyptians.'

Faruq Rahim shrugged.

'Egyptians or Germans, it doesn't matter much,' he said, 'so long as they can do the job.'

It was an answer that McKitterick might have given; but not Mahmoud.

'I've been talking to one of your inspectors.'

'Oh, yes?'

'A man named Fricker.'

'Fricker? Oh, yes, I know him. German. Very hard-working.'

'He certainly seems very committed to the Department.'

'Always has been.'

'He was responsible, I gather, for the proposal to arm the ghaffirs?'

'Responsible? I wouldn't say that. He certainly discussed the proposal in a report he drew up.'

'Who was responsible, then?'

The Egyptian back-tracked.

'I'm not quite sure who the suggestion initially came from. In a Ministry, you know, there are always several hands at work.'

'The suggestion came from higher up?'

'I wouldn't say that.'

He wouldn't say anything, thought Owen.

The Egyptian sensed his reaction and back-tracked again.

'I think they welcomed it when it was put to them,' he said.

'Who put it to them?'

'I think I can claim the credit. After it had been talked through inside the Department.'

'The idea did come from Fricker, then?'

'Yes, but it needed to be talked through. And of course his original idea was modified in the process. So it wasn't quite his concept that went eventually to the Minister.'

'I see. The Minister welcomed it, I think you said?'

'Yes. Not at first. He had some doubts about it.'

'Which were?'

'Cost.' The Egyptian smiled. 'Whether the British would accept it.'

'However, they did. And you, I understand, were given the responsibility for overseeing its implementation?'

'That is so, yes. It is, essentially, a provincial matter, and I am the one who deals with the provinces.'

'You have had, of course, experience of the provinces.'

'Yes.'

'At Minya.'

'Yes.'

'Where, in fact, the problem has occurred.'

'I'm not sure I accept that.'

'Where do you think it occurred? Here?'

'No, no. If there genuinely is a problem – and I'm not sure that I accept that – I suspect it occurred between Cairo and Minya.'

'On the voyage?'

'Yes. We do get pilfering.'

'Two hundred guns?'

The Egyptian back-tracked once more.

'That does seem a lot. In fact,' he said smoothly, 'that is one of the things that makes one doubt whether the problem is quite as you envisage. I suspect that in the end we shall simply find a clerical error in the paperwork.'

'To which no real loss of guns corresponds?'

'Exactly.'

'The reason for my being here is, actually, that I would like to check the paperwork.'

'It has, of course –'

'Yes, yes, I know. Been thoroughly checked already, both

inside the Ministry and by people from the Ministry of Finance. I don't expect to find anything different. But I have seen the paperwork at the Minya end and now I would like to be able to say I've seen the paperwork at this end, too. I wonder if you would give me the necessary authorization?'

'Well, yes, of course.'

'A written authorization, perhaps? Let's get this part of the paperwork right at last.'

He folded it and put it in his pocket.

'Thank you,' he said.

'I'm afraid I'm going to have to go down to Minya again,' he said to Zeinab.

'Again!'

He felt her flinch.

'It will be for the last time,' he said.

'All right.'

She turned away.

'It gets harder for me here all the time,' she said. 'Without you.'

Owen was sitting outside a café in the Ataba when he saw McPhee go by, riding home on his donkey.

The Ataba was, as usual, crowded. It was the terminus for both the new electric trains and the old, horse-driven, simple cart-like native buses, and passengers waiting for either milled about in the middle of the square. Also in the square were peanut sellers, loofah sellers, sugar cane sellers, pastry sellers and dozens of other sellers, including hundreds of men, or so it seemed to Owen, offering banned seditious newspapers. Not to mention camels, donkeys, chickens and Passover sheep. Unsurprisingly, the traffic, including McPhee, had come to a stop.

McPhee, tall anyway and with the advantage of his donkey, was able to look over the heads of the crowd. He caught sight of Owen and waved a hand. He seemed preoccupied, as well he might be in such a mêlée.

A surge in the crowd brought him up alongside the tables in the café. He looked down at Owen.

'Owen,' he said. 'I think, actually, that it's sheep.'

'I'm sorry?'

'Sheep. Not cats.'

'You do?' said Owen cautiously; and then, as that did not seem sufficient. 'Why shouldn't it be cats?'

'Because you can't eat them,' said McPhee triumphantly.

This was it. He had finally gone. He had been threatening to do it for some time. Now it seemed that something had snapped. Perhaps it was the Army call-up that had precipitated it.

'Well, no,' he said gently. 'No. That's very true.'

And then, after a pause:

'Why would you want to eat them?'

'It's not so much that, it's that you wouldn't want to feed them unless you *could* eat them. Not if you were very poor, as, of course, most Egyptians always have been. So they go for sheep.'

'Ye-es?'

Sometimes McPhee's strange mental processes actually led somewhere. Could that be the case here?

'As pets.'

'Pets?'

'I was thinking, you see, of our conversation down in Minya. At the cat cemetery.'

'Oh, I see.' He tried to remember. 'About cats, was it?'

'And whether the Egyptians looked on them as pets. I don't, on reflection, think that they did. They certainly don't now. It's sheep.'

There was some truth in what McPhee was saying. Many Egyptian families, even those in the city, did keep sheep. They fattened them up for Passover. And it was true, they did treat them as pets. They dyed their wool bright colours and decked them with pretty ribbons. And then they let them wander the streets, getting in the way of everybody, as they were doing now, here in the Ataba.

But –

'Cats, on the other hand,' said McPhee seriously, 'are a luxury. It would be all right if you were a temple. You wouldn't have to bother about the cost of feeding them,

181

people would donate food. There would be no economic problem. But for everyone else, for ordinary Egyptians, it *would* be a problem. So I was wrong in thinking they could be pets.'

'You are talking about the cats in the temple down in Minya?'

'And in the cemetery, yes. It was precisely because they were *not* pets that they could be singled out for veneration. They could not be absorbed into domestic life, not in the way, for example, that Passover sheep can. They were *other.* Yes, *other.*'

Owen considered.

'The German woman, too,' he said, 'was she "other"? Is that what you are saying? Was that why they put her in the cat cemetery?'

McPhee looked at him earnestly.

'You know, Owen, I think, in a way, that it was.'

16

The mudir met him with a great, beaming smile.

'Effendi,' he cried, 'you time your return well. All is ready for you. You can go to any village you want. You will find that everything is in order. The ghaffirs are as new. Talk to any of them! You will find them fine, upstanding men.'

'Simple?'

'Only a few, Effendi, only a few.'

'Old?'

'Not a dodderer among them! Well, one or two, perhaps, but then they'll bring experience to the job.'

'Blind?'

'Not very, Effendi. Most of them. No, Effendi, you will find them strong, stout-hearted men, I promise you.'

'They've all been properly elected?'

'They certainly have, Effendi. I've made sure of that. There's not an omda that's not felt the toe of my boot. And, Effendi . . .'

'Yes?'

'There's not a girl among them! How about that?'

'Excellent.'

'As a matter of fact,' said the mudir, 'there weren't that many. But there's no doubt that the idea was catching on. You were right to warn me. But there'll be no more of that sort of thing, believe me. Not now that I've had a word with a few people. No, Effendi, you can start when you like. We're all ready for you.'

Owen said there was a thing he'd like to check first in the accounts. The mudir waved a hand relaxedly and Owen went on to the small office, where the clerk was bent over some papers.

'Effendi?'

He jumped up.

'I'd like to consult your files once again, if I may?'

'What, particularly, would you like to see, Effendi?'

'The consignment note,' said Owen. 'The one for eight hundred and fifty guns that you worked to here at the Minya end.'

The clerk produced it from the filing cabinet and laid it before him.

Owen studied it for a moment, then folded it and put it in his pocket.

'Effendi!' said the clerk, shocked. 'You cannot take it away!'

Owen took it out again and spread it on the desk.

'You may make a copy,' he said, 'for your records. But the original, I keep.'

When he came out of the mudiriya a truck was waiting and in it was the mamur, relaxed and smiling. They drove out in the direction of the sugar cane factory, calling at several villages on the way. At each the ghaffir was indeed a fine, upstanding man; more than that, a real tough.

They called in at the village where he had seen the girl ghaffir. She was no longer there. Instead, there was a brawny individual with scars on his cheeks and what looked suspiciously like an old bullet wound down the side of his head.

'There!' said the mamur proudly. 'A real man, yes?'

The man grinned and touched one of the assembly of daggers tucked into the ammunition belt that ran from shoulder to hip.

'Gun?' said the mamur.

The ghaffir unslung it and tossed it familiarly to Owen. Owen caught it and looked at it. It was one of the new ones, all right. He squinted down the barrel. It was as shiny as any of the guns in the armoury of the barracks at Abbassiya. He handed it back.

184

'It's well kept,' he said.

'Of course it is!' said the man indignantly.

'An improvement, yes?' said the mamur, smiling.

'Well, you would think so,' said the omda surlily, 'but the girl was better.'

'Better?'

'At scaring away the crows. This bloke thinks it beneath him.'

'But you chose him?'

'Oh, yes,' said the omda hastily. 'At least, not I. The men of the village.'

'Dead right,' said the ghaffir.

Owen already knew that it would be a waste of time.

When they came to the sugar cane factory they changed to donkeys and set off along a track which led out of the village. At once the sugar cane closed about them, closing out the sky and light, closing in the heat. The tall canes, sometimes ten feet high, occasionally touched overhead. More often they had been cut back and there was a strip of blue sky above the track. There was never anything other than sky and cane, however.

When the cane touched overhead it was like going through a tunnel. The shade gave no relief from the heat, though. Instead, the cane seemed to trap it in, even when it had been cut back. Within seconds Owen's tunic was completely wet with sweat.

After a while they came to a village. It consisted of a few houses, some palm trees and a dovecote. The mamur ordered the ghaffir to present himself. A tough came forward, armed to the teeth. Owen inspected his gun, asked a few questions and they rode on.

They came to another village. Another tough.

It was the same at the third village. Only, while they were stretching their legs, after speaking to the ghaffir, Owen saw a small girl looking at him. Her face seemed familiar.

'Hello,' he said, 'you're not the ghaffir here, then?'

The girl removed her thumb from her mouth and grinned, pleased to be recognized.

185

'No,' she said, 'they sent me home.'

'This is your village?'

'That's right.' She pointed to one of the houses. 'That is where my uncle lives. He doesn't beat me now.'

'Not now that you've been a ghaffir?'

'Not now that I've got a gun,' she said.

'You still have it?'

She looked around, took him by the hand and led him off behind the houses. They were at once in the sugar cane. She stooped down and crawled along a kind of burrow among the stalks. At the end she felt in among the roots and pulled out a gun wrapped in leaves.

'There!' she said proudly. 'You can inspect it, if you like,' she said.

It looked pretty good to him.

'Didn't you have to give this back?'

'They didn't like to ask.'

Owen wondered what he ought to do. In the end he decided to do nothing.

They went back to the village, where the mamur was waiting for him. They mounted the donkeys and rode on. As he left, he gave the girl a wave. She took her thumb out of her mouth and waved back.

They plodded on all afternoon. The ground became rougher and the track narrowed. The great walls of sugar cane pressed in on either side. If anything it was even hotter than it had been before. By now it was late afternoon and the heat had had time to build up in the spaces between the cane. It reached up at him from the ground, closed in on him from the sides, gripped him as in a vice.

He was drenched with sweat. He could feel it running down inside his shirt, prickling inside his trousers where his skin rested on the donkey's back. He was riding in the Arab way, perched on its rump, his feet not dangling down but crossed in front of him over the donkey's neck. The donkey's movement was regular, almost soothing. He closed his eyes against the sweat and fell into a doze.

Occasionally he blinked them open. Whenever he did, he

would see the mamur's donkey ahead of him, the mamur nodding drowsily on its back.

It was taking longer than he had expected. The mamur had said that it was a matter of a couple of miles but perhaps he had been speaking loosely. Distance, though, in the sugar cane, was hard to judge. The sweat was making his eyes smart and he closed them again for a brief moment.

He came to with a start. The mamur's donkey was no longer in front of him.

The track ahead was straight for perhaps fifty yards. If he had fallen behind it must have been by a considerable distance.

He struck the donkey's flank and urged it forward. At the end of the fifty yards the cane bushed out slightly into the track, obscuring the view, and perhaps beyond that . . . But beyond that the track continued again, straight for almost a quarter of a mile, straight and empty. Surely he couldn't have fallen behind to that extent!

The mamur must have turned off some way back and not noticed that he wasn't following.

Owen cursed himself. He turned the donkey round and retraced his steps. There wasn't a turning off for quite a long time and when he looked along it, the track was empty.

He went on to the next turning, with the same result. Surely the mamur couldn't have turned off before that! Perhaps he had turned off after all at the previous track and got so far along it that by the time Owen had looked, he had disappeared from sight.

Owen knew that this was serious. The sugar cane stretched for a score of miles and in it you could get lost forever.

He decided that the reasonable thing was to stay on the track he had originally been on. He turned the donkey again and rode back up it, cursing himself.

What struck him now was the emptiness of the sugar cane. In the whole of their ride they had not come upon a single person or animal, much less a sign of human habitation. The cane stretched all around him, reaching up high overhead, and, to his unused eye, completely featureless.

He cursed again; not just himself but also the mamur.

187

He had been riding along the track for some considerable while now. If the village had lain ahead, surely he would have come to it.

Then a thought struck him. If there was no village ahead, there certainly was behind – the one he had originally come from. He hadn't been aware of them taking any side-turnings.

He wheeled the donkey again and set off back. The sun was getting low in the sky now. Before long it would be dark. Well, in a way, that didn't matter. He would continue as long as he could and then simply stop for the night. In the morning they would be looking for him.

All the same, it was vexing. He cursed himself for being a fool and cursed the mamur, too, again.

And then, suddenly, behind him, there was the sharp crack of a rifle.

The donkey jumped, and that probably saved his life, for there was another crack and this time he felt the bullet go past him, so close it seemed to touch his cheek.

He threw himself off the donkey and scrambled into the cane.

The donkey brayed with alarm and then ran off down the track.

Owen waited. And now he was cursing himself again, this time for a different reason: his folly in coming without a gun.

In Cairo he hardly ever carried a gun. If he thought one was likely to be needed, then he took one. But mostly, with his kind of police work, it was better not to. The violence that he was usually concerned with was that between ethnic groups, and talking was better than shooting in that sort of situation.

But this wasn't Cairo. It was territory infested by brigands, and he ought to have known better. Sitting peacefully chatting in Minya, or with the Schneiders, or with Mahmoud in the village, he had allowed himself to be lulled into a false sense of security, treating it as if he was on some kind of official trip.

188

But, hell, it *was* an official trip! It had been set up by the mudir, with the mamur as an official guide.

And then the realization came to him. Set up, indeed! This was a trip from which he was not intended to return. He had told the mudir too much.

He could see it all now. The mamur's disappearance had not been accidental. He was part of it. It had been his role to bring Owen out here and then somehow find an opportunity to take him out into the sugar cane and leave him where those more expert at the next bit than he could complete the job.

He knew that after a while they would come looking for him. He half-toyed with the idea of burrowing through the sugar cane back alongside the track and then coming up behind them, but he knew at once that this would be no good. There were at least two of them, armed very probably not just with guns but also with daggers, and he would never be able to jump the two of them together. His only hope was to wriggle deeper into the sugar cane and give them the job of finding him, to make the cane his ally not his enemy.

He began to crawl deeper. Each cane plant was separate and there was enough room for him to wriggle between them. However, the base of the plants was choked with under-growth; not just the thick, sharp-edged leaves of the cane itself, but also the mass of tendrils and vines that hung between them, often so thickly that he had to tear them apart.

But if it was hard for him, it would be hard for them. They would have knives, of course.

There was another thing, though, in his favour. It was getting dark. Once it was night, they would never find him. And in the morning there would be people out looking for him.

He inched his way deeper into the cane, away from the track. The problem, oddly, was not so much now the density of the undergrowth as the dust on the leaves, which rose up and threatened to choke him. Several times he had to stop because he thought he was going to gasp and they would hear him.

Once, they fired and he froze. But the bullet was nowhere near him and he realized that they didn't really know where he was, they were just firing at some false disturbance in the cane or else at random.

Lying there, deep beneath the cane, he could not tell how dark it was. It seemed to be getting darker, though.

There were one or two more shots, but these were certainly at random.

His hands closed on a large stone and he pulled it towards him. It was not much but better than nothing.

And now it definitely was darker. They would not be coming into the sugar cane to look for him now.

He stretched out and tried to make himself comfortable, listening for any noise. But there was no noise now, not even from the insects. There was just the fidgeting of the night crickets.

Later the moon came out and for a few moments he was alarmed because it was so bright that surely they would be able to see him.

But then the light faded and gradually the darkness changed and became the remote greyness of before dawn. He lay on, lay until it was grey no longer but bright sun, which he could see in speckles beneath the cane and which slanted through the leaves towards him. Only then did he begin to wriggle back towards the track.

He had decided that what he would do was to get as close to the track as he could and then lie there, still under cover, until he heard the searchers coming along.

It took him a surprisingly long time to get back to the track. He must have crawled further than he had supposed. At last, however, he could see the bright sunlight ahead of him. He lay and listened. He could hear nothing; no sound either of searchers or of brigands. He lay on, lay until he was sure that the sun was almost directly overhead. Then he wriggled forward.

He looked along the track in both directions. It was empty. He pushed his head and shoulder cautiously out into the sunlight.

And then there was a crack, and a stalk just ahead of him,

on the opposite side of the track, jumped and he heard the bullet winging on into the undergrowth.

He pulled his head back into the sugar cane. Almost at once there was another shot and this time it hit the cane directly above him. Another shot went into the cane a yard or two away from him, and then another.

He wriggled back quickly, going deeper and yet deeper. More shots came, but they were not close.

They knew where he was though. They knew, too, that he didn't have a gun. This time they would follow him in.

He could hear them now on the track. There was no longer any need for concealment. They fired again.

And then they were joined by another gun, from further along the track. It took him a moment to realize. It couldn't be firing at him. It was firing at them.

The men on the track near him began to fire back. Whoever it was along the track replied. In a moment a brisk exchange of shots was going on.

Owen was so relieved help had arrived that for quite some while he just lay there thankfully listening to the shooting.

Then he began to feel puzzled. There seemed to be just one gun further along the track. Whoever his friend was, he was on his own.

He felt worried. One man against two. And probably a man much less experienced at this kind of thing than the brigands were.

If only he had a gun!

But if he didn't have a gun, at least he had the experience. He began to worm his way through the undergrowth towards the solitary gunner.

The shots continued, in more desultory fashion now. But at least no one was doing what he was doing. Both sides seemed content to maintain their distance.

The occasional shots gave him a direction and even a rough indication of distance. It couldn't be far. They were firing by sight along the track, and the track, although straight, was not that clear.

He worked his way until he was parallel to the track, as

far as he could judge at right angles to his ally. Then he struck in, cautiously. He didn't want to be shot by his own side.

When he got to as close as fifteen or twenty yards from the track he stopped, huddled tight to the ground, and then called, softly.

There was a silence.

He called again.

No one answered. He waited and called again, but still there was no reply.

'Owen,' he said. 'The Mamur Zapt! Effendi!'

Nothing.

He decided to risk it.

'I'm coming forward,' he called, and then began to wriggle towards the track, keeping as tight to the ground as he could. Why the hell didn't they answer?

'Effendi!' he said again. 'Friend!'

A little way in front of him he heard something stir.

'Don't shoot!' he said urgently. 'I'm on your side!'

Then he worked his way forward, no longer trying to keep himself hidden.

He could see something, someone, lying close to the ground among the sugar cane roots.

'Come forward!' a voice said.

He stopped in his tracks.

It was a girl's voice.

Then he heaved himself forward.

'What the hell are you doing here?' he said.

It was the girl ghaffir.

'I saw you go,' she said, 'and I saw the donkey come back. The omda has sent to the sugar factory for help. But I thought I wouldn't wait. Haven't I a gun? I thought you might need me.'

'Never more have I needed anyone! Listen, there are two men.'

'I know. I saw them.'

'They are dangerous. We must take care. It is hard for one gun to fight against two.'

'That is what I thought,' said the girl. 'And therefore I hid in the cane and waited for them to show themselves, so that I could be sure I would kill them.'

'That was wise. But perhaps it is also wisest, it being one gun against two, not to try to kill them unless one has to, but to wait for aid to arrive.'

The girl considered. Her thumb went to her mouth.

She took it out again.

'The trouble is,' she said, 'that I think they advance. The last shots came from closer.'

'Then in that case we must make ready. How many bullets have you?'

'Two,' she said, showing him.

'Two!'

'One each,' she said.

'Enough, but only if one can be sure of hitting.'

'That is why I hide and wait.'

Owen took a deep breath.

'What is your name?'

'Na'ima.'

'Look, Na'ima, you are a mighty warrior and have fought like a true soldier. But I have fought for more years than you and know these guns as I know the back of my own hand. I think that, although you are sure of shot, I would be surer. Would you let me take the gun?'

The girl's thumb went back to her mouth. She considered for a long time. Then she took it out of her mouth again.

'All right,' she said reluctantly.

'Bless you, Na'ima!'

Where she lay was a good natural position and he saw no reason to change it. They lay there and waited.

For a long time nothing happened. The insects buzzed about their heads. The heat, in the dense undergrowth, was terrific. He had to keep wiping the sweat from his forehead. He didn't want it in his eyes just at the crucial moment.

Na'ima lay cheek to the ground, looking along the track.

She touched Owen on the arm and pointed.

He saw the movement too. It was on the opposite side of the track about twenty yards away.

They watched, and a few moments later it was repeated, this time five yards closer.

Another few moments, and another five yards, and this time he could see the man clearly. But where was the other man?

He showed Na'ima one finger and then put up two. She nodded, and then wriggled a little way away to get a different view.

Then things happened quickly. The man on the opposite side of the track appeared again, only now much closer, a bare five or six yards away, and this time, as he peered into the sugar cane, their eyes met.

Owen fired first.

The man fell, but then Na'ima screamed, and Owen, turning, saw the other man on their own side of the track. He fired and missed. The man's gun steadied.

And then a long, thin, black arm reached out from the cane behind him and pulled his head back, and another hand, holding a knife, came up and expertly cut his throat.

17

She was tall, very tall for a woman, over six feet, and quite black. Her face was long and her hair curly and clipped short. She wore only a loin cloth about her middle.

'Why did you do it?' asked Owen.

She stood there considering him. The flies were already buzzing around the man at her feet.

'I know you,' she said at last. 'You were there that day, that day when they raised her body. I saw you. I saw your face. It was like stone. They said you had come from the city to hunt them down, and I said, yes, I want a man like that, with a face of stone. But then you went away again and nothing happened for a long time. Then that other man came down, and they said that you were two dogs that hunt together, and I was glad, for I knew then that you had not forgotten my friend.'

'I had not forgotten her. I was following a trail in the big city.'

She nodded.

'I thought that might be so. For she came from the big city and it was reasonable to suppose there might be a trail there.'

'It is strange that she, coming from the big city, and you, a woman of the sugar cane, could be friends.'

She shrugged.

'We were women together,' she said.

'How did you meet?'

'Through her man. I was bidden to go to him and while I waited outside I saw her. She had little cats in her hands and was feeding them. And I went up to her and spoke to her, for I could see she would do no harm. And she did not, and spoke to me kindly. And after that I looked for her every time I came. And she for me, I think.'

'She was lonely; as perhaps were you.'

'We had both been cast out; she from her people, I from mine. She told me her story and I told her mine. We wept for each other. And yet our stories were not the same, for her man loved her.

'However,' she said, 'he did not love her as I loved her. To him, the little cats were nothing, but to me they spoke of gentleness. And I needed gentleness. I needed to believe again that there was gentleness in the world. Shall I tell you what a life is like without gentleness? It is like my life. I would not wish such a life on anyone.

'And yet it is not the worst life. The worst life is when they take everything from you and laugh. For then you know that it is no good being gentle, but that you have to be fierce, as fierce as they – no, fiercer. So I was fierce and I am glad of it. Afterwards, I fled, for there is no living with a people once such a thing has happened. I am not sorry; yet I knew that something was missing, and when I saw her, with the little cats, I knew what it was.'

'She meant much to you.'

'She was like the sun, which warms everything; or, since the sun here is unfriendly, like the moon, which shines even in a dark night.'

'It is right that you should mourn for her.'

'It is right,' she said, 'that I should take vengeance.'

'But do you know who it is on whom you should take vengeance?'

She hesitated.

'Tell me,' said Owen, 'what it is that you know.'

'One night,' she said, 'I was making my way home from the village. It was late and all were sleeping. I thought suddenly that I would like to see my friend. Not to speak with her, just to see her. And I went to her window and looked in. It was dark and I could see nothing, but that did not matter. It is easy for me to enter through windows and I thought

196

I would climb in and look at her while she slept and then go.

'Then I saw that there was a lamp lit in another room and I thought: "Perhaps she is there." But it was only the old woman, the mother. And I turned to go.

'But as I turned, I thought: "What is it that she is doing?" And I looked again. She was holding something white, and I thought at first that it was swaddling clothes, but then I saw that it was bandages, many of them. They lay all over the room.

'Well, I thought no more of it at the time. I decided not to go and see my friend after all but to continue on my way. It was only later, when I heard about my friend, and went down to the Place of the Cats to see her, that I remembered the bandages. For I knew at once that they had been meant for her.

'Still I was puzzled. For I did not yet know who it was I had to kill. Was it just the old woman? Or did others have a hand in this? And then the other man came, your friend, and then you, and I knew that you would find out. And so I waited.'

She looked at Owen.

'Now,' she said, 'you must tell me. I saved your life. You owe me a blood debt and must repay it. Tell me who killed my friend.'

For some time he had been aware of the truck coming. Now it came into sight. In it were Mahmoud, Schneider, the omda of the nearest village and several sturdy but apprehensive villagers.

Mahmoud jumped down. His eye took in the two bodies lying on the track.

'This one I can understand,' he said, looking at the man Owen had shot. 'But this one?'

'Some help from a friend,' said Owen, nodding towards the Cat Woman.

Mahmoud went up to her.

'I have been looking for you,' he said. 'There are things I would ask you.'

'I will tell you what you want,' she said. 'But, remember, you must also tell me. Your friend is bound by a blood debt; and, since you are his friend, you, too, are bound. I have required him to tell.'

Mahmoud nodded.

'What is it that you have required him to tell?'

'Who killed her.'

'That you may take vengeance?'

'Yes.'

'We are bound, and will tell,' said Mahmoud. 'But you will not take vengeance. That is for us.'

The Cat Woman was silent.

'She has an interesting thing to tell,' said Owen. He told Mahmoud about the bandages.

Mahmoud nodded. He did not seem surprised.

'I think it best if you come with us,' he said to the Cat Woman. 'You were her friend and it is right that you should hear.'

They all climbed up into the back of the truck. The villagers meanwhile had thrown the bodies in.

'Thanks for coming,' said Owen. 'How did you know?'

'The omda sent a message,' said Mahmoud. 'When your donkey came back without you.'

They stopped at the village to let the omda and the villagers get down.

The girl ghaffir got down with them.

'You will be looking for a new ghaffir,' said Owen. 'May I recommend this one? As a fighter, she has no equal.'

'And I can scare away the crows,' said the girl, taking her thumb out of her mouth.

Owen saw that she now had two guns slung over her shoulders.

He left it at that.

Schneider was driving and Owen and Mahmoud were in the cab with him.

'Yes,' said Schneider, 'of course I knew about the brigands. But they didn't interfere with me so I didn't interfere with them. In this job you've got to live and let live.'

'Did you know about Hanafi's contacts with them?' asked Mahmoud.

'I guessed. But I didn't inquire too closely. It was between him and the mudir.'

'You should have done something,' said Mahmoud.

'What? Go to the authorities? The mudir was the authorities.'

Schneider stared out through the windscreen.

'You've got to make accommodations,' he said.

'With the mudir?'

'Yes.'

'The brigands, too?'

'A bit. Money, mostly. On the whole, they left us alone. It was the villagers that they were interested in.'

'They paid protection money?'

'Yes.'

'You should have done something,' Mahmoud said again.

'What could I do? They'd got the whole area stitched up. They and the mudir between them. There wasn't anything anyone could do. The brigands controlled the whole district. They put in the ghaffirs, of course. Every one. It was their way of controlling the villages. As time went by, that didn't matter so much. They grew careless, put in anyone. Even a girl.'

'And the guns?'

'The guns were for them. The brigands. They could pay for them. In fact, two hundred was more than they needed, so they gave them to their ghaffirs as well. That made it look as if they fitted in with the general policy.'

'Who did they pay?' asked Owen.

'The mudir. And whoever was in it with him. It was the kind of thing he did.'

He looked at Owen.

'You know what?' he said. 'Fricker was right. The brigands were an army and you needed another army to root it out.'

'There'll be another army,' promised Owen. 'Only it won't be a ghaffir one.'

*   *   *

199

When they got back to the sugar factory, Mahmoud asked if he could speak to Hanafi. He came out to them in the yard, looking nervously up at the bodies in the back of the truck. Schneider had asked Mahmoud if he wanted anything done with them, but Mahmoud said no, he would be taking them into Minya very shortly; that is, if Schneider could spare the truck just once more and find a driver. Schneider said he would drive them himself and then hung around until Mahmoud made it courteously clear that he wished to speak with Hanafi alone.

Not quite alone, in fact; with Owen, and also with the Cat Woman squatting down on her heels against the wall.

Hanafi caved in at once.

'I was the man who went between, yes,' he said, head bowed. 'The mudir came to me one day and said: "You live out in the sugar cane. I want you to take a message for me." But when I heard who the message was for, I said: "No, no, these are bad men. They will kill me." "They will not kill you," said the mudir, "they will reward you." But still I would not go. But then the mudir said: "I know how it is with you. You need money, and then you can go to some other place where things will be better; Cairo, perhaps, or Alexandria. For that you need money. If you do what I say, you will be given money. And all I ask is that from time to time you carry a message."

'Well, I thought about it, I thought long and hard. It was true I needed money. I could see no other way of getting away from this place. My family . . . they would not be so bad if we were in another place, a bigger place, where there were more people, where they would not be all.

'We had to get away. Things were becoming harder all the time. For her. I could see it, I knew it. We had to get away. I had brought her to this place, it was I who had done this to her. I had to do something. And all it was, was taking a message. So in the end I took the message.'

'And other messages.'

'And other messages, yes.'

'And did you get paid?'

'Not enough. Not enough to be able to leave this place.'

'The mudir would give you the message, you would come back here to the factory. And then?'

'I would wait for her,' said Hanafi, looking nervously towards the Cat Woman.

She gave a little, mirthless smile.

'How did you know when to come?' Mahmoud asked her.

'He would tie a cloth to a tree,' said the woman, 'and I would see it on my way back from the village. I came to the village often.'

'To steal?'

'That is so,' she agreed.

'And then she would guide you?' Mahmoud said to Hanafi.

'Yes.'

'How did you know where to find them?' Mahmoud asked the woman.

She shrugged.

'Are you with them?'

'No, I go my way, they go theirs. But I know where to find them.'

'And you didn't?' Mahmoud said to Hanafi.

'They move all the time.'

'So you contacted her. How did you do that? The first time?'

'There were people in the village.'

'They would put out food for me,' said the Cat Woman.

'I knew that she knew the sugar cane,' said Hanafi, 'and would be able to find the brigands.'

'And so, with her help, you went between the mudir and the brigands,' Mahmoud said to Hanafi, 'and took their messages. You will say this in a court of law?'

'Yes,' said Hanafi quietly.

'Good. Another time I shall ask you about the messages. But now there is something else I wish to ask you about. You know, I think, what it is.'

'Yes,' said Hanafi.

'Shall I help you? You wished to get away and could not. You were tied to this place. And she was tied to you, and

201

you to her. And your family knew this, and could see only one way out.'

'No!' said Hanafi. 'No! It is not true what you are saying!'

'Did not your mother buy the poison?'

'It is true that she bought poison,' whispered Hanafi, after a moment. 'But that was for the cats. It was not for my wife. How could it be? They had lived long together in one house without harming each other. Why should one suddenly wish to kill the other?'

'I can think of many reasons,' said Mahmoud. 'First, although they had lived long together, they had not lived well together. Second, a mother is always jealous for her son and if she feels a wife is harming her son, she may feel wrath towards her. Your wife had borne you no son. Doubtless your mother urged you to set her aside or marry another woman, and, doubtless, too, you refused. So what was to be done? Third, you had chosen your wife from another people, whose ways were not as your ways. Between your wife and your mother there was argument. She did not own your mother's authority in the way that she felt she should. Well, I can think of other reasons, but these are enough.'

'They are not enough. My mother would not have done it. It is true that they did not live well together, that there was difference and much argument. True, yes, that we had no child and that my family wished me to divorce her. But all this was nothing if I deemed it so.'

'Now, is that true?' said Mahmoud quietly.

'Yes!' said Hanafi defiantly. 'I am the eldest son and in the household it is as I command.'

'I do not think so,' said Mahmoud, shaking his head.

Hanafi flushed.

'It is so!' he insisted.

'I think not.'

The Cat Woman laughed.

Hanafi looked at her angrily.

'Your mother, I think, gives the word in the household,' said Mahmoud.

'On small things: on the day-to-day of the household, yes.

But not on big things. Over the piano, for instance – there I commanded. And it was so on this. She does not go against my word.'

'But in that case,' said Mahmoud, 'you have to explain how it is that she *did* go against your word.'

Hanafi stood gasping like a fish.

'She was seen,' said Owen, 'with the bandages.'

'Or perhaps,' said Mahmoud, 'she didn't go against your word?'

Hanafi stood there for a long time. Out in the middle of the yard, the heat was intense. The Cat Woman crouched by the wall. Like a coiled spring, Owen thought suddenly. He moved round to where he could intercept her. Schneider had come to the door of the factory and stood watching them curiously.

'It was not like that,' said Hanafi at last.

'What was it like, then?'

'One day I came home from the factory,' said Hanafi. He was almost inaudible, 'and found her sick. She was crying. She said she was a burden to me, and that there was no way out, that our attempt to make a life together had failed, and that she was only making things worse for me. And so she had tried to end it.'

'How?'

'By taking poison. There were some pills I took when I had headaches. She thought if she took enough of them then that would do it. But it didn't. And then she took something else which made her feel sick. But sick only, nothing more.

'And I said: "God be praised!" But she said, no, there was no other way and, and that she would try again. I remonstrated with her, I pleaded with her, I spoke of us and all we had meant to each other. But she wept and said it was of no use, that we had tried to be together but that the world would not have it so, that the world was too strong for us.

'I argued with her, of course I argued with her. Again and again. But I could not reach her. Always in the past, when she had been depressed, I had been able to reach her, but this time I could not.

'And I knew she would do it. She was always stronger than I was. So I said: "You shall not do this alone. If we cannot live together, at least we can die together." At first she would not have it. This time it was she who argued. But for once I was firm.'

'And?' said Mahmoud.

Hanafi swallowed.

'I spoke to my mother. I said: "She has decided to end it." And I told my mother to get poison and put it in her bowl. Only in her bowl, for I knew that if I told my mother it was for both of us, she would not do it. But I meant to see that I took it too.'

'Well?'

'She did as I commanded. And got the poison and one day she put it in the food. And Hilde ate.'

'But you did not?'

'I did eat!' said Hanafi brokenly. 'But not enough. I saw her suffering and rushed to her. I could not bear to see her suffer. And then I tried to eat the rest but my mother took away the bowl and would not give it to me.'

'So she died,' said Mahmoud, 'and you did not.'

'I did not mean it so. I would not have had it so. I looked for some other means to kill myself but my brothers held me. And then I fell into a daze. I could not think or speak. I lay as one dead. I lay like that for hours.'

'And meanwhile your mother saw to it all?'

'Not in the way I would have wanted,' said Hanafi hoarsely.

'The bandages?'

Hanafi nodded.

'And the place,' he said. 'She should have lain with her own people.'

'She should not have lain alone,' said the Cat Woman.

'I should have died,' said Hanafi, sobbing. 'I wished to.'

They took Hanafi back with them to Minya. At the mudiriya they got out and Owen handed Hanafi over to the friendly constable he had met on the waterfront.

Then they went in to see the mudir.

204

'You?' he said, his eyes almost starting out of his head when he saw Owen. 'You?'

Mahmoud hustled the mamur in at the door.

'You stupid bastard!' roared the mudir. 'You've got it wrong!'

'He certainly has,' said Owen. 'And so have you.'

'This man said he had lost you,' said the mudir, with a swift attempt at recovery. '"Lost!" I said. I don't mind telling you, Effendi, I hit the roof. "Lost!" I said. "You can't lose an effendi! Least of all, the Mamur Zapt!"'

'That's right,' said Owen.

'This foolish fellow! But, Effendi, don't judge him too harshly. He's hopeless in the sugar cane.'

'That's right, boss,' said the mamur hastily. 'Don't know my ass from my tits.'

'An accident,' said the mudir. 'Pure accident! I was going to send out a search party. We had just spoken about it, hadn't we?'

'That's right, boss.'

'"Get on to it straightaway!" I said. "Or else –"'

'"– you'll feel the toe of my boot,"' said the mamur mechanically.

'That's it!' said the mudir, beaming. 'Effendi, how can I express –'

'Don't bother,' said Owen. 'We know all.'

'We have Hanafi,' said Mahmoud.

'Hanafi!' said the mudir, his beam fading. 'A man of no account –'

'And therefore fit for your purpose,' said Owen. 'He went between you and the brigands; and you could always disown him if he got caught. Did he carry the money too?'

'Money?'

'The money the brigands gave you for the guns.'

'Effendi, I told you there were no guns –'

'I have seen them. And been on the wrong end of them.'

'Effendi –'

'I know how they were picked up from the end of the jetty. I know, too, how the notes that went with the delivery were switched. And I know, too, who at the other end, in the Ministry, drew them up. I have writing in his hand. It matches the writing on the false consignment note. You did this together, as you had always done things together. But as always the first idea came from him. When Fricker Effendi presented his report he saw very quickly how it could be turned to advantage. Monetary advantage. For you and for him.'

18

Kitchener was not coming back.

As always, the Mamur Zapt, Head of the Khedive's Secret Police and one who moved in the highest of places, was the last to hear it. The news was halfway round the bazaars by the time it reached the British Administration and even then it reached Owen only via Zeinab.

'Have you heard?' she said excitedly as he came through the door. 'Al-Lurd is going.'

Owen did not think this was likely.

'It's true,' she insisted. 'He is to join the *cabinet* of the King's favourites.' 'Cabinet' was not quite the same as Cabinet and His Majesty's Ministers would hardly designate themselves as the King's favourites; nevertheless, this began to sound more plausible.

'In what capacity?' asked Owen cautiously.

'He is to command all the King's armies.'

'Secretary for War?'

'War, certainly. I don't know about Secretary. I think he's higher than that.'

Even then Owen was not entirely convinced.

'Where did you hear this?'

'Leila told me. Fawzi was there and she had heard it too. And then Nazli came in –'

There could no longer be any doubt.

The British Consul-General, the man who had been the real ruler of Egypt, had gone.

Cairo was buzzing with the news. The next morning, as soon as he stepped out on to the street, the water seller accosted

207

him with it. The people buying newspapers at the kiosk were talking about it. The old lady who sold oranges from a heap in the road called it out to him as he passed, the donkey-boys squatting round the large tray of a pavement café looked up at him and asked his views.

Arabeah drivers at a nearby rank clustered round him and asked what difference it would make to Egypt, and the policeman on traffic duty held up the traffic – which at that hour in the morning amounted only to a surprised water-cart spraying the sand to keep the dust down and two camels carrying firewood to the hotels, which ignored him anyway – to discuss it with him.

At the tables outside the cafés it was being bandied around among the office effendis taking their early-morning coffee; and when he entered the orderly room at the Bab-el-Khalk it was the first thing the orderlies said:

'What about this, then, Effendi?'

At the bar in the Sporting Club that lunch-time it was the sole topic of conversation.

'Just when I'd got him trained,' complained Paul. 'How could they do a thing like this without consulting me?'

It hung in the air at every meeting; and this was particularly true of the meeting he attended late that afternoon.

It was the first meeting of the committee that Cavendish had spoken about and which he had now set up. It included, as well as Cavendish himself and Owen, Paul, representing the British Administration, two staff officers from the Army, and also two archaeologists, one of whom Owen did not know but who appeared to have done a lot of travelling in Mesopotamia, the other, the bumptious Lawrence. Owen did not think they were there because of Cavendish's interest in archaeology.

When Owen arrived, they were talking about the imminent entry into the war, on the German side, of Turkey, which they all seemed to take for granted. What was worrying the Army was the possibility that Turkey might take advantage of Kitchener's departure and time its declaration of war to coincide with an invasion across the Suez Canal.

'But surely you're prepared?' said Paul.

'Of course we're prepared!' snapped one of the officers. 'But is everyone else?'

'What kinds of civil preparation are you thinking of?'

'Well, the disarmament of the population, for a start.'

'Daggers? Clubs?'

'Guns,' said the other officer. 'If what we hear is true.'

'What do you hear?'

'That there's an illicit native army operating behind our lines.'

'I think you can discount that possibility,' said Owen.

'But can we? Are you sure?'

'Captain Owen has been looking into this very matter,' said Cavendish.

'So we understand. But how far has he got?'

'There is no army,' said Owen.

'But there has been a considerable leakage of guns?'

'Yes.'

'That is very worrying.'

'Not very. But it is part of a wider picture that has been causing me some concern.'

He told them about the issuing of guns to the ghaffirs.

'Ghaffirs?' said one of the officers incredulously.

'Guns?' said the other officer. 'New service rifles?'

'What sort of numbers are we talking about?' asked the archaeologist whom Owen did not know.

'Ghaffirs. Fifty thousand. Not that many guns yet.'

'Fifty thousand! Bloody hell!' said the officers simultaneously.

'I agree that it is cause for concern,' said Owen, 'and therefore I have some proposals to put before you. I think we should call the guns in.'

'Too bloody right!'

'Fifty thousand!'

'It would mean overruling the Minister,' said Paul.

'Well, isn't that unfortunate!'

'Look, there's a war on, isn't there?'

'I can see Mr Trevelyan's point,' said Cavendish thoughtfully. 'It would draw attention to the ambiguity of the British

position in Egypt. Which might not be a good idea just at
the moment.'

'And therefore I am suggesting that the call-in takes a
particular form,' said Owen, 'one that will not require us to
overrule the Minister or even change policy. The Ministry
accepts that a number of guns have gone missing. What I
suggest is that, in order to establish exactly how many, we
require all the guns that have so far been issued to be checked
in at local control points. Since the Ministry bears some of
the responsibility for the loss of the guns, it can hardly object.'

'Yes, but – '

'The guns will be held until the process of checking and
counting is completed.'

'But that would be only a temporary solution,' objected
one of the staff officers.

Owen smiled.

'In Egypt,' he said, 'things can sometimes take a long time.'

Lawrence came up to Owen at the end of the meeting.

'How many guns did you say there were?'

'Fifty thousand at most.'

'Fifty thousand!' said Lawrence thoughtfully. 'I could do
a lot with them.'

The Army was so relieved that it readily agreed to send a
detachment south to put down the brigands.

Faruq Rahim, that agile climber of the bureaucratic ladder,
had at last put a foot wrong and was sent to a place where
he could disappoint his colleagues no longer.

Cavendish came across to him in the bar.

'Good work!' he said. 'You'll be invaluable on the committee.'

'Well . . .'

'You know,' said Cavendish, 'I've been thinking. You'll be
needing some help when that strange Scotsman has gone.
I'll see what I can do.'

'I wonder, actually, if he is quite the right chap for the

210

Army,' said Owen. 'He would be of much more use here.'
'You think so?'

Paul appeared alongside Owen a little while later. He, too, had been thinking about the recent changes.

'First, Kitchener; then McPhee. They are robbing us of all our talent. I expect to be next.'

'As a matter of fact, I wanted to have a word with you about my own position. Have you had a chance to –?'

Paul shook his head.

'Not a hope!' he said. 'Cavendish has put an absolute veto on it. You're much too valuable here, he says.'

Owen went to see Fricker.

'You have found the missing guns? That is good!'

He seemed genuinely pleased. He had, he said, been worrying about it. Owen thought it was like Fricker to worry about someone else's administrative problem.

He shrugged when Owen told him about the decision to make the ghaffirs hand in their guns.

'Circumstances change,' he said, 'and we in administration have to change with them. Perhaps after the war –'

Owen told him about the Hanafis. Fricker listened in silence.

'So,' he said after a while. 'So.'

He asked if it would be possible to write to Hanafi. Owen said it would.

'Would you mind,' Fricker said, 'if I wrote it now and gave it to you? The new commandant does not allow correspondence. I asked him why and he said it was against Regulations. I asked him if I could see a copy of the Camp Regulations but so far he has not replied.' Fricker seemed puzzled. 'I thought, perhaps, I could make one or two suggestions –'

Owen went for a walk round the camp while Fricker was writing his letter and thought that perhaps when he got back to Cairo he might make some suggestions of his own.

Fricker was just sealing the envelope when Owen returned. He stopped.

211

'Perhaps I should not –? You may read it if you wish.'

Owen said it wasn't necessary. He took the letter and put it in his pocket.

Fricker thanked him formally.

Afterwards, he stood there for a moment.

'I have been thinking,' he said, 'and perhaps, after all, I do understand it. They loved each other so much that they could not bear to be parted. I think that was partly because they were afraid. Afraid of what might happen if they *were* parted. Would their marriage survive? And if it did not survive, what would become of them? As individuals?

'They had become so dependent on their marriage, you see. They had invested so much in it. Everything. They had given up everything else for that – music, career, their families, society. And they had put it all into their marriage.

'And now they were beginning to wonder if they had been right. They *had* to have been right or else everything was meaningless. They could not risk having to face the possibility that they had been wrong. They had to stick to their marriage, it was all they had.

'And then when it seemed that it was going to be taken away from them –'

'Taken away?'

Fricker looked at him in surprise.

'Well, yes,' he said. 'Hilde was German, you see. Like me.'

'I don't see,' said Zeinab.

'She would have been taken into internment,' said Owen. 'They could see that was going to happen. And then they heard that I was coming down. That's what precipitated it. They thought it was the end. Of everything. So why not end it themselves? Together.'

He was silent for a moment. Then he said:

'You want to know who really killed her? I did.'

'Not you. Internment. The war.'

'You can't divorce administrative processes from people,' said Owen.

Zeinab didn't say anything for quite a while. Then she said:

212

'It wasn't just a marriage of love, it was a marriage of fear. Perhaps it wasn't like that to start with. It was just love. But then as the world pressed in on them and they didn't seem to be able to hold their own, fear began to come into it. The outside world was too strong for them, there were too many obstacles, difficulties, so they turned inwards. In the end they couldn't face the world; so when the world came calling . . .'

She looked at him.

'We wouldn't be like that,' she said, 'if that's what you were thinking.'

'No.'

'And, anyway, it wasn't even the world, it was war. And you're not going to the war now, are you?'

'I'm just afraid it might come calling,' said Owen.